On This Journey of Life What is it Costing You!

Diana B. Andrus

ISBN:1717201287
ISBN-13:9781717201287

DEDICATION

This book is dedicated to everyone who wants to pursue their dream; with God all things are possible. God has given each of us a gift.

CONTENTS

ACKNOWLEDGMENTS

I would like to thank God for making this possible. I want to thank friends and family for standing by me through this time. I have worked very hard at writing this book and I hope it impacts your life in some way.

1 Everything You Do Will Cost You Something!

There is lying, cheating, and stealing in this short story. Jonathan was a man with a known past. He thought things for him would never get better so he kept doing the same things. When Jonathan realized that a changed mind is one of his strengths; that is when things began to change for him, but before then he had to hit rock bottom. There is a saying, "If you keep doing the same thing, you'll keep getting the same results." Jonathan had plans but he was in for a rude awakening. One neighbor was married and one neighbor was a widow. The married woman was devilish, but the widow was full of wisdom. Sometimes in life we settle, but everything you do in life cost you something. Look around and see some of the things that sin will rob you of. When we make a decision it's either for the better or worst; there is no in between. It's a High Cost for Low Living! You might want to weigh your options!

One day Jonathan was sitting around thinking about all the things that money could buy. Jonathan thought, "It won't cost me anything if I steal", even though I'm taking a chance." Well Jonathan started making plans on how to do this money thing. See Jonathan came from a very bad environment and thought there was no hope for him. He had already been to jail several times and this time would not be any different, so he thought. Well he thought his plan thru and went over to the neighbor's house two doors down. Now Mrs. Raney was married, but her husband worked out of town. As Jonathan approached the door to knock, Mrs. Raney opened the door. See, she saw him coming. Mrs. Raney was a very flirtatious person, but only when Mr. Raney was not around. She had her eye on Jonathan for a long time; I think he knew that too. Well as he entered the house, Mrs. Raney was very polite, "Have a seat if you like." Jonathan slouched down on the sofa. I believe that is what turned Mrs. Raney on. Well, as the evening went on; they shared a few glasses of wine and talked. Several hours have passed and Jonathan decided that it was time for him to go. He did not want things to be too suspicious; he was really scoping the house out; so he thought. Well as he approached the door, Mrs. Raney asked him would he like to dance; he told her; "You are a married woman", she replied,

"What Mr. Raney won't know, he don't have to know." Jonathan said, "I guess one dance won't hurt anything." Mrs. Raney put on a slow song, but Jonathan was not comfortable with that so she changed it to a swing-out song. As they danced, all of a sudden Mrs. Raney pulled Jonathan into her chest. She began to kiss Jonathan's neck and Jonathan tried to resist her but the temptation was too strong. One thing led to another and Mrs. Raney and Jonathan ended up in the bedroom. Well, after it was all over, Mrs. Raney was still acting very frisky and told Jonathan, "we will meet again on next week." Jonathan has a smirk on his face as if; this is now alright to continue. They smooched for a bit and Jonathan left out of the front door. Well Mrs. Nosey from across the street just so happen to come out the same time Jonathan was leaving Mrs. Raney's house. She yelled, "Jonathan, can I see you for a minute?" As Jonathan approached Mrs. Nosey, she noticed he was a little nervous. She said, "I just wanted you to know if you would like to start mowing my lawn twice a week?" Jonathan said, "sure and I appreciate you asking me". Now Mrs. Nosey was a lonely old widow who just wanted company because her husband has been dead over 15 years. Jonathan only thought that he was going there to mow her lawn, but Mrs. Nosey had something else in mind. Well, Jonathan went home with a smile on his face from Mrs. Raney and Mrs. Nosey.

Well the next morning, there was a knock at the door, it was Mrs. Nosey. As Jonathan opened the door stretching, Mrs. Nosey said, "Could you come and mow my lawn? Before Jonathan knew it, he said, "sure"; not realizing it was only 6:30 a.m. Jonathan found it very strange that Mrs. Nosey came over even though she already told him about her lawn on yesterday. Well, as Jonathan was getting ready to go to Mrs. Nosey's house, the phone rang. It was Mrs. Raney calling to see if Jonathan could come over; she had something she needed him to look at. Jonathan explained that he was about to mow Mrs. Nose's lawn. Mrs. Raney abruptly hung up the phone. Well, Jonathan did not pay it much attention, but thought it was strange for Mrs. Raney to do that. As he walked across the street, he could almost feel someone staring at him, but he never looked back. Well when Jonathan arrived at Mrs. Nose's house, she had everything set up for him to begin mowing her lawn; Jonathan was very impressed. Time passed along as Jonathan mowed; Mrs. Nosey kept him refreshed with lemonade and snacks. Well, Jonathan finally finished mowing. Before he left, Mrs. Nosey invited him inside the house; she wanted to discuss something with him. Jonathan sat down on the sofa and Mrs. Nosey sat right beside him. His mind went back to when he was at Mrs. Raney's house so Jonathan politely got up and moved to a chair. Mrs. Nosey politely told him, "You don't have to be afraid of me; I have been around a long time and have seen many things in my lifetime." Mrs. Nosey noticed a very strange look came over Jonathan's face, like guilt. Mrs. Nosey said, "I saw you across the street at Mrs. Raney's house on yesterday; I know her husband is not there because he works out of town." I just want to let you know that just because the opportunity is there does not mean you have to take it because everything you do in life will cost you something. Jonathan went on to say, "What are you; Mrs. Nosey interrupted him and said, "Just remember what I told you." Mrs. Nosey paid Jonathan the money for mowing the lawn and Jonathan went home. As Jonathan crossed the street, he felt as if someone was staring at him, he looked back, and it was Mrs. Nosey waving good-bye. Jonathan waved at her as he entered his house. As soon as he sat down to watch the news, the phone rang; it was Mrs. Raney. She insisted that Jonathan come over because she needed him to fix something for her. Well, he paused a minute then said, "It will be over shortly". After the news went off, Jonathan went over the Mrs. Raney's house. When Mrs. Raney opened the door, she had on this sheer dress with black lining;

Jonathan's eyes were fixed on the dress. As he entered, she offered him a seat. Jonathan said, "What is it you need me to fix?" Mrs. Raney said, "I have been so stressed out since my husband been gone and I need a massage." Jonathan was kind of shocked because he thought she really needed something fixed. Well, Jonathan being the kind of guy that he was started massaging Mrs. Raney's shoulders, but for a second thought about what Mrs. Nosey said earlier. That thought did not last long with Jonathan, he and Mrs. Raney end up in her bedroom again. Afterwards, Jonathan told Mrs. Raney: "This can't keep happening because you are married." Mrs. Raney said, "My husband is never here so I need someone while he is away." Jonathan then asked, "What is in it for me?" Mrs. Raney said, "I will compensate you for your time." Jonathan had this big grin on his face and he said, "Cool." Jonathan ignored Mrs. Nose's advice and did not give it a second thought. As Jonathan opened the door to leave; there was Mrs. Nosey sitting on her porch looking straight in that direction. Jonathan turned his head and went to his home without acknowledging Mrs. Nosey. Even though he did not say anything to Mrs. Nosey, he is reminded that, everything you do will cost you something. Jonathan at this time did not know what that meant, but it will come to reality in his life.

As the evening dawned; Jonathan was watching a movie on television; it was about "Cheating Spouses getting caught." He found that topic very appealing. He watched the movie until he fell asleep on the sofa. Well, the next morning, Jonathan went out and sat on his porch listening to the birds chirping on a hot Saturday morning. As usual, Mrs. Nosey was already out on her porch. As he looked over, he noticed that Mr. Raney's car was at home. About 15 minutes later, Mrs. Raney and her husband came out to get into the car; Jonathan noticed that Mrs. Raney did not look in his direction not once, but Mr. Raney waved and Jonathan also waved. Later that day, Mrs. Raney and her husband returned to their house with bags of groceries. Mrs. Raney had about 3 bags in her hand. All of a sudden, one of the bags fell out of her hand, immediately Jonathan ran over to help. Mr. Raney was inside taking the other bags in the house. As Mr. Raney came out of the house, he noticed Jonathan was face to face helping Mrs. Raney pick up the bags that she had dropped. Mr. Raney said, "Um, what is going on?" Mrs. Raney said, "Jonathan came over to help me because I dropped the bags." Mr. Raney had this strange look on his face and said, "I will take those bags if you don't mind." As Mr. Raney went back inside the house, Mrs. Raney said, "You shouldn't have come over here, you are making my husband suspicious." Jonathan immediately left without saying anything.

Well, it was Sunday and Mr. Raney normally leaves out to go back on the road. Well, Mr. Raney for some reason decided to stay later than he normally stays. Mrs. Raney was kind of suspicious as to why he has not left to go back to work yet. She just patiently waited and finally about 2 hours later, Mr. Raney left to go back to work. Mrs. Raney was worried about the way Jonathan left abruptly on yesterday. Mrs. Raney picked up the phone and called Jonathan, and she asked Jonathan if he would he come over for a little while; Jonathan agreed. As Jonathan left his house to go to Mrs. Raney's; he noticed Mrs. Nosey had her porch light on. It signified to Jonathan as if somebody's watching you. Well as Jonathan approached the door, he saw a car light coming down the street. He began knocking abruptly because he did not want anyone to see him going to Mrs. Raney's house this late. Mrs. Raney opened the door and Jonathan went inside. They had their glass of wine as usual and danced for a little while. Well, for some reason Jonathan felt uneasy; I guess because he has never been there at night. As the night progressed, they were getting a little tipsy; things were getting a little out of hand. Jonathan and Mrs. Raney went upstairs to her room;

leaving the music playing down stairs. Mr. Raney drove about 30 miles away and realized that he had forgotten his wallet. He tried calling the house so Mrs. Raney could meet him and he would not have to drive all the way home. Mr. Raney called several times, but no answer; he found that very strange being he just left home. Mr. Raney decided to turn around and drive back to the house. Mrs. Raney and Jonathan came back down stairs and Mrs. Raney noticed the answering machine flashing; she played back the messages and realized Mr. Raney was on his way back home. Her heart began racing and Jonathan immediately said, "I have to go before your husband gets here." Jonathan and Mrs. Raney talked about when they would meet again. As Mrs. Raney opened the door, she seen headlights; it was Mr. Raney turning into the driveway. Jonathan said, "How will you explain this to your husband." She said, "I won't, you will have to hide." Jonathan hid in the hall closet as he heard Mr. Raney turn the key. Mrs. Raney went as if she was about to unlock the door; but Mr. Raney opened the door. He immediately said, "Where were you, and why didn't you answer the phone?" She said, "I was in the shower washing my hair, sorry I did not hear the phone." That's when Mr. Raney told her he left his wallet. He asked Mrs. Raney, "Have you seen my wallet, it was sitting here on the hall table." She began helping her husband look for his wallet, but could not find it. Mr. Raney then said, "I will call my supervisor and let him know that I will leave tomorrow after going to the Driver's License to get me a new driver's license. Mrs. Raney could have fell dead knowing Jonathan was in the hall closet. It was the longest night that anyone could ever have, Jonathan thought. As Mr. Raney went upstairs to take a shower, Mrs. Raney told him she would be up in a minute. Mrs. Raney immediately opened the hall closet and told Jonathan, "Hurry you must leave quickly." As she let Jonathan out the front door, she noticed a package in his back pocket; it was her husband's wallet. She could not address the matter at that time; she just needed him to get out of her house. When Jonathan made it home, he looked across the street at Mrs. Nosey's house and noticed the porch light was still on. He remembered, her saying, "Everything you do will cost you something."

The very next day after Mr. Raney left to go back to work; Mrs. Raney telephoned Jonathan to come over, but Jonathan did not answer his phone. Mrs. Raney decided to go over to his house. Surprisingly, Jonathan was not at home. Mrs. Raney found that very strange. Well, a few hours passed by and Mrs. Raney saw Jonathan come home. She immediately went there to approach him about her husband's wallet.

She said, "Jonathan did you take my husband's wallet?" He said, "No; I have no reason to take anything from you, but what you give me." She knew he was lying, but could not prove it. Mrs. Raney left Jonathan's house very upset with him. Mrs. Raney called Jonathan once she got home and told him, "I no longer want to see you." Jonathan told her, "You don't have a choice or I will tell Mr. Raney everything. " Mrs. Raney felt as if she was trapped. Later that week, Mr. Raney called and stated that the credit card company has notified him that someone has been using his Visa card. Mrs. Raney was stunned; she told Mr. Raney to call and cancel all his cards.

Mrs. Raney and Mrs. Nosey have been neighbors for a long time. They never visited each other, but today Mrs. Nosey decided to go to Mrs. Raney's house. Mrs. Raney was glad to have a visitor after what Jonathan has done. Mrs. Nosey told Mrs. Raney that she has seen a lot in her lifetime. Mrs. Raney had this puzzled look on her face. Mrs. Raney began crying and began telling Mrs. Nosey about her and a young guy who she has been having an affair with. Mrs. Nosey gave Mrs. Raney this advice," You tell your husband, before he finds out." Mrs. Raney said, "I can't hurt my husband like that." Mrs. Nosey said, "He is already hurt, he just doesn't know it." Mrs. Raney said, "I don't understand why this is happening to me, I was just lonely." Mrs. Nosey said, "Everything you do will cost you something." Mrs. Raney thought about everything Mrs. Nosey said and decided she would tell her husband everything. Well it was approaching the weekend and Mrs. Raney was getting very edgy. She took it upon herself to talk to Jonathan about the situation again. She called Jonathan and asked him to come over; she told him she needed to speak with him. By this time, Jonathan knew that Mrs. Raney was on to him. Once he arrived to Mrs. Raney's, she was her usual self. She offered him wine, but Jonathan refused; he was there just to see what Mrs. Raney wanted to talk to him about. Mrs. Raney felt the coldness of Jonathan so she had to go a different route with him. Mrs. Raney noticed Jonathan had on new jeans and a shirt. Mrs. Raney said, "You look very nice today." Jonathan immediately said, "Cut to the chase, what is the reason you called me over here." Mrs. Raney began explaining that her husband's wallet was still missing and someone has begun charging on his credit cards. Jonathan said very snobbish, "Why are you telling me?" He said, "Oh, because I have on some new clothes, you think that I have your husband's credit card." Jonathan said, "I have been mowing Mrs. Nose's yard for several weeks now." Mrs. Raney had a very curious look on her face and then said, “I have never seen you out there mowing her lawn.” Jonathan told Mrs. Raney to call Mrs. Nosey while he was sitting there, so he could prove his case. Well, Mrs. Raney called Mrs. Nosey and she vouched for Jonathan. Mrs. Raney immediately apologized to Jonathan for accusing him. Mrs. Raney could not believe this was happening when she saw the wallet in his pocket; she had to figure out another way to prove Jonathan had her husband’s wallet.

Early the next morning Mrs. Raney got up and sat at the kitchen window looking in the direction of Jonathan’s house. After sitting there for quite some time, Jonathan finally came of the house with a bag and went walking down the street. Mrs. Raney decided to follow Jonathan to see exactly where he was going. She really believed that Jonathan had taken her husband’s wallet. He went into this tall building and went inside this room where a lot of people were meeting. She did not want to look suspicious so she went back to the car to wait on Jonathan to come out. As long as she knew where the place he was going, she would come back another day and check it out. Jonathan stayed in there for about an hour or so. After he left there he went back home. Well to keep Jonathan from getting suspicious to see him and Mrs. Raney getting home at the same time, she decided to go back to the place.

When she walked through the doors, she saw all types of people there. After standing in amazement for a while, a gentlemen approached her and said, “May I help you?” Mrs. Raney said, “What type of place is this?” The young man said, this is a place where people with AIDS get tested on a monthly basis. Mrs. Raney’s eyes got so big and her voice started trembling. The young man said, “Are you o.k.?” She just turned around slowly and walked out in a daze. All kind of thoughts were going through her mind like, “Do I have AIDS, Do my husband have AIDS?” She finally got home and as usual Mrs. Nosey was sitting on her porch, but noticed that Mrs. Raney was not herself. After Mrs. Raney went inside, about 5 minutes later Mrs. Nosey knocked on the door. Mrs. Raney said, “Come in”; she did not get up to open the door. As Mrs. Nosey entered she noticed Mrs. Raney was in deep thought. Mrs. Nosey asked, “Is there anything I can do for you?” Mrs. Raney began crying and Mrs. Nosey went and held her. After Mrs. Nosey settled Mrs. Raney down, Mrs. Raney told Mrs. Nosey that the young man that she has been having an affair with has been getting tested for AIDS at the center downtown. Mrs. Nosey said, “Is it Jonathan?” Mrs. Raney said, “Yes”. Mrs. Nosey said, ‘What are you going to do?” Mrs. Raney said I must speak with Jonathan first. Later on that evening, Mrs. Raney decided to call Jonathan over to discuss this matter. Jonathan thought it was going to be the usual thing.

When Jonathan arrived at Mrs. Raney, she did not offer him wine and she did not have any music on, it was just quiet. Jonathan said, "What's on your mind?" She said, "Do you have AIDS?" Jonathan looked with this blank stare on his face; he said, "What makes you ask me something like that?" She said, "I followed you this morning to see if you were going to the store ". He then said, "You still think I stole your husband's credit card?" Mrs. Raney told him he went to the AIDS center and wants to know if he has AIDS. Jonathan stayed silent a long time, and then he said, "YES". Mrs. Raney burst out crying. She then said, "Why didn't you tell me?" He said, "I tried, but you were so aggressive things got out of hand. She said, "My life is over once I tell my husband because we both will have to be tested." Jonathan said, "When are you going to tell him?" She said, "Soon." As they were talking, the phone rang, it was Mr. Raney. Mrs. Raney put her hand over her mouth to let Jonathan know not to say anything. She held the phone as Mr. Raney was talking to her and she began crying. She told him she had something to tell him. He asked if it could wait until he gets home this weekend; she agreed. After hanging up, Jonathan sincerely apologized and told her that he has been positive for the past 2 years and that it was not his intensions to pass it on; he slowly walked out of the door with his head down. Mrs. Nosey seen Jonathan and said, "Hi there, can I talk to you a minute?" As Jonathan sat on the porch besides Mrs. Nosey, she put her arm around him and said, "Son, do you remember the words I told you the very first time we talked?" He said yes, "Everything you do will cost you something". He said, "At first I had no idea what that meant but I understand now." Mrs. Nosey said, 'Were you going to tell Mrs. Raney about you having AIDS, he said, "No". Mrs. Nosey expected that answer from Jonathan because he portrayed that in his character. Mrs. Nosey was a person of wisdom and she told Jonathan, "If you would have told the truth, it would have cost you something, but you told a lie and it has cost you everything." Jonathan looked puzzled and said, "What do you mean by that?" She said, "Not only does this disease take your life, but you have taken someone else's life." Jonathan said, "I never thought of it that way." Mrs. Nosey let Jonathan know that she knew he had a hard life growing up, but there is always room for change. Jonathan then said, "How Do I Change?" Mrs. Nosey told him one day at a time. She told him he needs to get it right with Mrs. Raney and her husband. Mr. Raney has a right to know what is going on. He said he will do it the weekend. Well the weekend had finally come, as Jonathan sat on the porch, Mr. Raney pulled into the driveway. This was Jonathan's chance to come clean with the Raney's. Jonathan said, "Mr. Raney can I speak with you for a minute." He said, "I know we did not get started on a good note, but I really need to speak with you and Mrs. Raney." Mr. Raney said, "Could you tell me what it is about?" Jonathan said, "I rather not say at this time." Mr. Raney said give me about 30 minutes to freshen up." Jonathan went home and he was contemplating on what he was going to say. Well, the phone rang and it was Mr. Raney calling for Jonathan to come over. Mrs. Raney answered the door and was shocked to see Jonathan. She said in a whispering voice, "What are you doing here?" Mr. Raney said, "Is that Jonathan honey?" She said, "Yes, are you expecting him?" He said, "Yes, he needs to talk to you and I." Jonathan came and set down on one sofa and the Rainey's on the other. Jonathan started off by saying that he has never been at a point in his life where he wanted to do things right for first time. He said, "First of all, I want to return your wallet." Mr. Raney looked and said, "How did you get my wallet?" Jonathan said, "That is the other thing that I want to talk to you about." As Jonathan began to talk, Mrs. Raney interrupted him and said, "Honey that is what I been trying to tell you; I have been having an affair with Jonathan and he has AIDS." Immediately Mr. Raney stood up and Jonathan stood up and said, "If you want to hit me, go ahead." Mr. Raney said, "Just get out." Mrs. Raney began crying hysterically. After Jonathan left, he could here Mr. Raney yelling at the top of his voice. Well it seemed as though daylight would never come. The next day Jonathan went out to set on his porch when he noticed Mr. Raney had his trunk up and was taking clothes out of the house. The phone rang and it was Mrs. Raney. She said," Mr. Raney wants a divorce." Jonathan told Mrs. Raney he would go out to speak with him, but it was too late because Mr. Raney had already left. Weeks has passed by and Jonathan and Mrs. Raney had not spoken neither had Mr. Raney come back home. About two weeks later Jonathan noticed a strange car was sitting around the corner; it kind of made Jonathan nervous since he had a criminal record. Mrs. Raney had become distant since all this has happen.

About two weeks later, Jonathan had a knock at the door; it was an undercover detective. He needed to talk to Jonathan regarding Mr. Raney's complaint. Mr. Raney filed a complaint regarding you knowingly having AIDS. The detective said he needed to take Jonathan downtown.

As Jonathan and the detective were leaving; he asked if he could go to talk with Mrs. Nosey. The detective said, "You have 5 minutes." Jonathan knocked and Mrs. Nosey came outside. Jonathan told Mrs. Nosey that he thank her for all the advice she have given him. Later that evening the detectives brought Jonathan back home after questioning him regarding deliberately infecting the Raney's with the disease. Jonathan knew that he was innocent until proven guilty. He told Mrs. Raney he knew for 2 years, but she would have to prove it. Eventually, Mr. Raney came back home and decided he was going to work the marriage out. They became very distant from Jonathan since all this has happened. Mrs. Raney knew that Jonathan told her, but how would she trap him to confess to it; that is the only way he would go to jail for a long time. So many things began to go through Jonathan's mind. He remembers telling Mrs. Nosey how he wanted to change, but then he felt if he could get away with this he would. Weeks had passed by and as Jonathan sat day dreaming on his porch, Mrs. Raney came over and asked if she could speak with him. She apologized for everything that has happened. She also told him that she did not know her husband pressed charges. Mrs. Raney said, "If it would help, I would tell the police that you tried telling me, but I was too aggressive and you never got the chance." Jonathan said, "You would do that for me?" She said that is the least I can do since I did come on to you." Mrs. Raney said she would talk with her husband and see what he said. She said, "Mr. Raney acted out of anger and rage." Jonathan said, "I understand because I don't know what I would do if someone done such a horrible thing to me." As Mrs. Raney walked away, she said, "Jonathan you are a good person and sometimes good people do bad things." That thought stuck in Jonathan's head. He said to himself, "I'm not a bad person, I just done a wrong thing." That was the beginning of change that Jonathan told Mrs. Nosey he wanted to do.

Jonathan started going to Mrs. Nose's house on a daily basis because she had a lot of wisdom. One day Jonathan asked Mrs. Nosey, "How do you know so much?" She said, "I don't know anything, but God knows everything; it is he who has given me wisdom to know things. Jonathan said, "I have heard of God, but how do you get to know him?" Mrs. Nosey said," through his son Jesus." Jonathan had a smile on his face like never before. Mrs. Nosey said, "I have never seen you smile like that." Jonathan said, "If this Jesus has given you all this wisdom and long life, I know he will give it to me." Mrs. Nosey smiled and said, "I see the change coming." Mrs. Nosey told Jonathan that he first needed to accept Jesus as his Savior. Jonathan said, “I’ll do anything to get to know Jesus.” Jonathan was on his way to recovery. Well Jonathan accepted Jesus and was converted. Mrs. Nosey told Jonathan that Bible Study was on Monday nights and he is welcome to go with her. Jonathan began going to Bible Study with Mrs. Nosey. Jonathan became like a son to Mrs. Nosey. As time went on, the Raney’s were going on with their day to day activities. Jonathan was so focused on his new salvation, he had almost forgotten about the charges that were filed against him. Later that week, Jonathan got a letter in the mail to appear in court for the charges filed by Mr. Raney. Jonathan was so filled with the Holy Spirit and built up on the word until he was ready to face whatever was coming his way. The morning of the court, Jonathan stopped by Mrs. Nosey before he left. He asked her to pray for him and she said, “How about I go with you.” Jonathan just put his arms around Mrs. Nosey and said, “Thank you, I would like that. As they arrived at court, they seen the Raney’s; they waved at each other and went into the court room.

The court was in session and the lawyer asked Jonathan did he know he had Aids at the time he slept with Mrs. Raney? Jonathan said, “Yes, I knew.” The judge looked with a face of amazement; he could not believe his ears. Well, they took a break to come back in for the ruling of the case. The judge said, “I have heard statements from Jonathan and also Mrs. Raney came into the chambers and told me some disturbing news that, she came on to Jonathan and did not give him a chance to defend himself." The Raney’s had a heart of compassion since they have seen a change in Jonathan. The Judge stated, “This would be somewhat an easy case to rule on, but it is something peculiar about this young man. I have looked up his record and he has a long past of wrong doing, but I must say a change has taken place in this young man; he went on to say; “I have no choice but to set him free.” Jonathan immediately stood up and said, “Thank you Jesus.” He hugged Mrs. Nosey and ran over and hugged the Raney’s. Well, a few days had passed by and Jonathan had to continually get blood work done at the office. Jonathan went back to the office to do a final Aids test. Mr. Tate called Jonathan into the office and said," son I have some good news; we have made a big mistake regarding the blood work. We have one other person here with the same name as yours. It has come to my attention that you are not HIV positive. Jonathan said, "Thank you Jesus". Jonathan rushed out of the building to go home to spread the good news. Jonathan called Mr. and Mrs. Raney and also Mrs. Nosey to his home. He told them he had some good news and he wanted to celebrate. Well, everyone arrived and Jonathan said, "There has been a big mistake at the center where I do blood work; somehow a student nurse got my name and the other person with the same name mixed up. I don't have AIDS. Everyone begin screaming and hugging with a sigh of relief. Jonathan then said, "I want to make a special presentation to Mrs. Nosey; "I want to take the time out to thank you for taking time up with me; you are just like a mother to me." "Not only did I get to know you, but I got to know Jesus through you." God put people in your life for a reason; to get you to another level, a season; to learn from your mistakes, and a lifetime to tell someone else about Jesus. Don't ever think that you are getting away with anything because your sins will find you out. There is a quote about sin: "It takes you further than you want to go, it makes you stay longer than you want to stay, and makes you pay more than you want to pay." Jesus is the only person that never done anything wrong and it cost him everything.

2 Day in Our Lives

Cloudy, Rainy, Stormy, and Sunshine

The Sun will Shine Again

Even though the sun is bright there will be days in our lives that are not so bright. It's not going to stop the sun from shining so we need to keep shining. The shine that we have may bring light into someone's darkness. Sometimes there is going to be some rain in our lives, but remember the sun was shining before the rain came. Make a decision to look beyond the rain. The day was going so well for Shelton when all of a sudden it became very cloudy and dark. All of a sudden Shelton's mood changed. He did not know what was happening to him. His supervisor approached him and said, "Shelton, are you alright?" He then stated, "I don't think so." His supervisor told him to go home for the rest of the day. As Shelton slowly walked away, he began to tear up and say, "I just don't understand why I'm feeling this way; like I lost my best friend. Shelton did not realize that the weather changed his mood. As he headed out the door, an old classmate yelled, "Shelton, "how are you doing", but Shelton kept walking never hearing her. After checking out with the cashier, she walked fast to catch up with Shelton. He was just about to unlock his car door when she made contact with him by touching his hand. He was startled and said, "Oh, Hi Sylvia". She said, “I spoke to you earlier, but did not hear me. Shelton said, "I was in deep thought.” The clouds were moving and the sun began to peek out again. Sylvia asked Shelton, "Would you like to talk about what is going on with you?" Shelton said, "I don't know where to begin. She said, "How about from the beginning." After Shelton shared his feelings with Sylvia, he realized that he was whelmed with life itself. It wasn't until it got dark and cloudy in his life to realize that he was in a depressed state and if the light would have not shown up through Sylvia, he may have been too far gone to turn around. Sylvia went on to tell Shelton; "In our lives we will have rainy days, cloudy days, stormy days, but through it all the sun will shine again." After hearing those words, Shelton was on his way to a new purpose in his life. He told himself, "No matter what life throws at me, I will look beyond the clouds and the rain and see the sun. You never know what a person may say to you that may change your life forever. So whenever you may go through a tough time in your life, always find someone to talk to.

[3] "Forgiveness"

What is forgiveness? It is a decision to change your mind about something that has caused you hurt and pain. In this life we will be hurt by those we know and those we don't know. When that time comes, will you be able to forgive that person for the wrong they have done to you?

Life has a way of bringing things to your door. Stacey and Steven had been married for many years. Stacey was a very private person when it came to her home affairs. As time went on, people began to notice that Stacey has not been quite herself lately. Normally, she would be off to herself and withdrawn, but now it seems she is beginning to mingle a little more. One afternoon Stacey called her friend Patricia to see if they could meet for lunch. Patricia and Stacey have been best friends for years. When they met for lunch, Stacey had on sunshades and jeans as usual. The funny thing was that she kept the glasses on; Patricia thought that was strange. Patricia being the person she was said, "Stacey, why are you still wearing your sunglasses in the building?" Stacey, said "Oh you know just one of those days." Patricia asked, "Is something going on with you?" Instantly, the glasses came off and Patricia could see that Stacey had been crying. Stacey said, "I can't take it anymore, Steven is a horrible individual." "I have been struggling with this for years and I just have to tell somebody." For the past few years my children and I have been verbally abused by my husband." Patricia immediately came and put her arms around Stacey to comfort her. Patricia assured Stacey that she will be there for her no matter what. As Stacey and Patricia said their good-byes, Stacey said, "I promise I will keep you informed." As time went on things at Stacey's home would go back and forth from better to worst. One morning Stacey had awaken out of her sleep and went to the window, she saw Steven outside as if he was planting flowers; all she could see was his back; so she went outside, but out of sight where he could not see her. As she got a little closer, she realized that he was praying. She could not really hear what he was saying, but the tears began streaming down her face. She realized that he realized the situation had gotten really bad and he had no one to turn to but God. By this time Stacey had become bitter towards Steven. See, in life everything start off as a raindrop and if we don't take care of the raindrops the situation will turn into a flood; and water out of control is dangerous; It could destroy everything. Just like fire, it is good for cooking, but out of control it will burn up everything. Stacey had been contemplating on leaving Steven, but could never do it. Steven and Stacey have both professed to be Christians, but sometimes our actions does not represent God. When we let ourselves become bitter, we are almost at our lowest. Anger will cause you to get a person back in the flesh. Well, Stacey knew she could not move on with her life without forgiving the things that her husband has done to her. She has really been struggling with this. While studying the word of

God; she thought about how God forgave her for her sins and how she had hardened her heart against her husband. When God saved us he put everything of his kind in us in order to deal with life's situations, but we have to choose to do those things. Stacey began studying her bible on forgiveness and she realized it was very painful to forgive all the wrong that Steven has done. It was because she was trying to forgive him in the flesh. Forgiving a person has to be done in the spirit. We don't have any strength in the flesh. Stacey and Steven had become very distant due to their situation; God was dealing with both of them. Stacey did not realize that Steven was struggling with past situations and did not know how to deal with it. When we try to change ourselves we just end up right back where you started; but Steven had to find this out for himself. Steven has been doing everything in his flesh which is where your emotions are. He even believed in his own strength in prayer. Sometimes what you see with your eyes can fool you. Just like the saying, "A picture is worth a thousand words."

As time went on Stacey began to pray more about her situation. She really began to confide in her friend Patricia, but she thought to herself, "I realize people will get tired of you, but God never gets tired of you." That is when she really started seeking after God for an answer.

She realized that unforgiveness has drastically changed her life. It has changed the way she talked and her attitude toward others. Everyone knew Stacey as this loving, kind, and caring person that would help anyone, but she became depressed with a made smile on her face. She now realizes after getting into God's word that she will never be the same if she doesn't forgive Steven. She asked God, "How do you forgive someone that has done you so wrong?" God spoke to her spirit, "The same way I forgave those who crucified me." She said, "But it is so hard God." He then spoke to her, "Trust in me and not in yourself; when I saved you I gave you everything you need to survive in this life." That was a life changing moment for Stacey. As she pondered on what the spirit had spoken to her, she said "Wow that had to be Love." She knew then that she had to forgive Steven based on what God said and not her flesh. This was going to be a real challenge for Stacey. Every morning she began to get up and seek God for guidance. Well throughout life we will learn that if we do things our way we will get our results, but when we do things God's way we will get his results. As time went on they could still feel the tension in the house as they were in each other's presence. In order for things to change, Stacey had to do what God told her to do. Stacey began doing the things a wife should do regardless of what Steven did. Love will melt the hardest heart. Stacey had to do it from the heart to be able to genuinely forgive Steven. Well as time went on, Steven began to say a little at a time to kind of break the ice. He knew that Stacey was very bitter the last time they had spoken. As Stacey began to say something to Steven, she felt a release in her spirit letting her know it was o.k. and that she was o.k. Steven had this look on his face because he was expecting something different from Stacey. As weeks went on Stacey decided that she and Steven needed to talk about their current situation. Being the person that Stacey was she decided to let Steven speak first. Steven started off by saying, "I know that we have had our differences in this marriage and I want it to get better so we can move on." Steven just did not know how much power his words had. Stacey said," Is there anything else you need to say before I began?" Steven said, "Oh, and I do Love you." Stacey was use to that sarcastic tone of Steven. Anyway, Stacey began by saying, "I would like to apologize for any wrong doing that I may have caused in our marriage to bring us to this point." She said, "I saw you the other morning praying in the yard." Steven had this smirk on his face as if he was off the hook. She said, "I have been praying too and seeking God regarding forgiveness." I'm now to the point to ask you to forgive me for the wrong I have done to you." Steven immediately said, "Well I was wondering when you were going to admit to being at fault for most of this." Stacey could feel her flesh rising, but she stayed calm and remembered what the spirit of God spoke to her earlier; "Put your trust in me." "Stacey went on to say, "I have forgiven you for all the wrong you have done to me and I'm now free to let you move on;' Steven said, "No I don't want to move on, I love you." Stacey said, God is love; and until we can love the way God says love; we haven't loved at all. See the forgiveness I have shown to you is not for you but it's for me.

4 *"FROM STRUGGLE TO SUCCESS"*
Sub Title: "Power in a Name"

Victoria is an 18 year old young lady who is struggling with fears in her life based on the way she grew up. Her parents struggles to make ends meet, but she decided to make a change in her own life. She found out her name means Victory and that gave her the boost she needed to make things happen in her life. You must always remember a change is for better or worst!

There is light at the end of the tunnel

Growing up poor in a large city has always been a struggle for Victoria; she grew up with parents and siblings, but it has always seemed like everything remained the same and nothing was going to change. Victoria lived in a very diverse neighbor. Everyone lived there was barely making ends meet or ends were not being met at all. Things at home had gotten pretty bad; they were down to one vehicle. Each day her father had to bring her mother to work on his way to work. Her mother had to ride the city bus home when she had the money; if not she had to walk until someone knew her would offer her a ride home. Victoria was a senior in high school and she attended "Gotta Go High School." Victoria grew up going to church and Sunday school. She participated a lot when she did attend church and Sunday school. Each day she would walk to school which was about 7 blocks from her home. Normally there are several people from the neighborhood walking to school together, but this particular day, she walked alone. About 4 blocks into walking to school she saw a piece of paper on the ground, so she decided to pick it up. The paper read: "How to Face Your Fears". She began reading this particular passage and below there was a contact number if you were interested in this program. Victoria continued to school with the thought of calling the number on the pamphlet. While in English class, the teacher wanted each student to write an essay on something that they feared the most. The minute Victoria heard this, she knew immediately that she must call this number and pursue this gut feeling that she had inside. She now knew that this was the right thing to do; free of charge. After school was over; she began walking home and a small voice said, “Look at the address”. All of a sudden a smile came on Victoria’s face because she realized the place was in route of going home. There was a problem, the center closed at 4:00 p.m. and it was already 3:30 pm. Victoria did not know exactly where the place was, but had the address. Victoria began walking extremely fast to get to the place. She then came upon the address and it was about 3:58 p.m." As she approached the door, she could see a lady in there so she pulled on the door; it was locked. Victoria began tapping on the window to get the lady's attention. The lady signified that they were closed. Victoria raised up the paper and said, “Your pamphlet said you close at 4:00 pm. and it’s only 3:58p.m. The lady gestured again, that they were closed. Victoria began to walk away slowly with her head down, all of a sudden she heard the door and she turned and looked back. The lady was waving for her to come back. When she reached the door, the lady said, “I normally don’t’ do this for anyone, but it is the calmness of your personality that really touched me," Victoria said, "I really appreciate this." The clerk said, "I'm Ms. Dorothy." Victoria went on to say, "I'm Victoria." Ms. Dorothy, then said, "Victory". She said, "No it's Victoria." Ms. Dorothy said, "I know, but your name stands for Victory. " Victoria said, "I never knew that." Ms. Dorothy said, "Victory means, triumph, success, accomplish." A bright smile came upon Victoria's face and she then said, "That means I can do anything I set my mind to." Well, Ms. Dorothy said, "What is your reason for coming to this program? Victoria said, "I want to overcome my fear of being poor." Ms. Dorothy allowed Victoria to fill out the paperwork to join the program. She was also given the days and times of the program. Victoria will begin the program on tomorrow. As Victoria walked home, she was so full of joy, but then a damper came over her when she realized that she had to tell her parents. They were very strict on her because so much has happened in the past in their neighborhood. She then realized that she was 18 years old and her parents could not really stop her from joining the program, but she was going to ask them anyway out of respect. As they sat down to dinner, Victoria said, "Mom, Dad, I have some news to tell you." The parents looked at Victoria and said, "What is it Victoria?" She told them that she joined a program to help her overcome fears that she has been facing. The room became silent for a moment, and then her father said, "I'm proud of you for doing that because I never got a chance to overcome my fears; I struggle from day to day wondering if I will be able to provide for this family." Then her mother said, "I'm proud of you also." Victoria then said, "May I be excused, I need to thank God for you as parents and then for blessing me with an opportunity to change things in my life." The wife looked at the husband and said, "Remember how we use to pray and go to church and look like things were better?" They agreed that they will begin to take time to pray and go to church on Sunday's.

The next day Victoria got up, doing her normal routine but this time she prayed before she went to school. She was chipper and cheerful all day and people took notice of it. Immediately after school Victoria headed to the new program. As she walked in the setting, she noticed people starring at her and she starring at them. This was a very unusual feeling for her. She found her a seat mid-way and the instructor entered the room to begin the session. The instructor had everyone introduce themselves at the end of the class. They will partner off with someone that has the same or similar reasons for being there.

Well at the end of the session, Victoria partnered off with Valor; she was a 19 year old drop-out. The teacher instructed them to find out what each other's name mean and to express it in their next session. Valor and Victoria left after session was over. Victoria said," I will give you the meaning of my name; triumph, success, accomplish. "Valor said my name means: courage, bravery, and boldness. They looked at each other with excitement and both said, "We are good for each other." Now Victoria and Valor had to decide which one would present the presentation to the class on tomorrow. Victoria being the person she was, decided to give Valor the opportunity to speak on their behalf. Valor rather Victoria do it, so it was settled. They parted their ways and went home. The next day came and it was time for Valor and Victoria to present their presentation for the meaning of their names. Victoria stood before 20 people and told them what the names meant. She said, "Victoria means Victory and Valor means Boldness. You must have boldness to have the victory and you won't have victory without boldness. To sum it up, they need each other to get through their fears. Victory and boldness must work together in order to succeed. The teacher stood and gave a standing ovation saying, "Job well done." Victoria and Valor hugged each other because they were so proud of themselves. They stayed and listened to the rest of the groups present their presentation also. As they left the center, they were getting to know each other better; they were becoming the best of friends. As Victoria arrived in the house, her mother and father were watching a television program. They said, "Well, how did things go with the program." Victoria said, "I met this girl name Valor and we partnered off and gave the meanings of our names and received a standing ovation from our instructor." She went on to say, "I'm glad you allowed me the chance to make a change in my life." Her father then said, "Your mother and I have decided to begin praying and attending church like we use to." Victoria's face lit up, and she said, "I know already it's getting better for us."

Well, early the next morning, it was raining out and only having one car, Victoria was wondering how she would get to school. Her father said, "Victoria would you like me to take you to school on my way to work?" She quickly said, "Yes, I would like that." As she and her father drove down the rode, he said, "I just want to thank you for giving me and your mother the boost we needed to get back on the right track." Victoria replied, "The only thing I done was prayed for our situation in our household to get better and it is day by day." Well, today was the day to present her presentation in English class titled, "Facing your Fears of Growing up Poor." Victoria stood up with boldness to present her essay. The class was in awe at the things that Victoria said, were very thought provoking. After class, she had people coming up to her letting her know she done a great job. You could tell in most of the student's faces that they felt bad for the way Victoria grew up, but Victoria was getting pass that stage. Each day she was getting stronger and stronger. This was a great Friday for Victoria; she went home and told her parents the good news. On Saturday morning Victoria's dad woke her and her mother up to go have breakfast at the diner. This is something they have not done in a very long time. While driving to the diner, her father said, "I have great news; I got a raise on my job." Her mother got teary-eyed because she could see the change in their lives already. Victoria said, "That is wonderful. " Well, when they arrived at the restaurant, there were these two men sitting at the bar. The two men said, "Good morning." Everyone spoke and we proceeded to our table. The waitress came to get our drinks and she said, "The two men at the bar wanted to know if you were new in town because they had not seen you in here before." Her father said, "No, we live about 5 miles down the road, we just have been having a hard time making ends meet, but things are looking better." After the waitress went back and relayed the message to the two men, they told the waitress, "We will pay for their food." After they ate their breakfast, they told the waitress they were ready for the bill, she stated, "your food is already paid for." The father got speechless and said, "How is that possible?" The waitress said, "The two men took care of the bill." Victoria's mother said, "No one has ever done anything like that for us before." You can see the thankfulness in their eyes and hear it in their voice. They wanted to thank the two men, but they had already left the restaurant.

Sunday morning had finally come; Victoria was up and ready to go to church, but the house seemed very quiet. She thought about what her parents said about going back to church. She went into the kitchen to get a quick bite to eat, as she looked in the den there were her parents dressed and ready for church. Victoria's face lit up and she said, "I did not know if you were up already." Her father said, "We wanted to see the smile on your face when you seen us." As they were on their way to church, there was an accident about 5 blocks down the road. Her dad let out a big sigh saying, "The very day we are trying to do the right thing something happens." Victoria said, "Don't worry, the traffic will be moving in a moment and we will make it to church on time. "

Sure thing as they passed by the accident, her dad looked with a deep concern. He said, "that look like the two gentlemen that paid for our breakfast on yesterday." Victoria's mother said, "It couldn't be; that would be too spooky." Well, they finally arrived at church, but before the pastor began to bring forth the message, he said he had an announcement to make. He said, "Brothers Bob and Billy were in a vehicle accident on their way to church this morning but we don't know the extent of their injuries at this moment." Victoria's father had a look of terror on his face because he actually did see them. The pastor decided to take about 15 minutes to pray for the two brothers. Victoria's father decided he wanted to pray amongst her and her mother. He said, "Lord Jesus, I ask to protect and keep Brothers Billy and Bob; they done a good deed by blessing us with food on yesterday; you said in your word that you reap what you sow, they have blessed us and now we are asking you to bless them." As they agreed in Amen, Victoria and her mother were wiping the tears from their eyes. Her father said, "That really felt good, I know they are going to be alright." After the church service, Victoria's family went spoke to the pastor and he gave them the hospital information and the telephone number to those who was concerned about the two brothers. As they left the church, her father said, 'Would you and your mother like to stop by the hospital? They both agreed. They arrived at the hospital and went to the nurses' station. The nurse gave the room number; by them being brothers, they put them in the same room. As they walked into the room, there were excitement in Bob's and Billy's eyes; they said, "Hey, it's the family from the diner." Her father shook their hands and Victoria and her mother gave them a hug. You could feel the love in the atmosphere. Bob asked, "How did you know we were here?" Victoria's father said, "The pastor told us." Bob said, "How do you know our pastor, he said, we belong to that church, but we haven't been in a few years. Well, they went on talking and getting to know each other. Finally, it was time to leave; they exchanged numbers and promised they would keep in touch with each other besides seeing each other at church. When they arrived at home, Victoria called Valor and told her all about her day with her family. Valor was excited for Victoria. Victoria then asked Valor where she attends church, and she said she doesn't. Victoria told Valor anytime she wants to go, she is welcome to come on Sunday mornings and ride with her and her family. Well it has been a long day so they said their good-byes and hung up the phone.

The school year was dwindling down and Victoria was about to graduate in a few weeks. Her classes at school were down to a ½ day so she started going to the program earlier in the day. Mrs. Dorothy asked Victoria what was her plans after graduating; Victoria said, "I haven't given it much thought." Ms. Dorothy told her that the center will need a new director after she retires in a few months. Victoria said, "Are you asking me do I want the position?" Ms. Dorothy said, "Since you are doing so well, they would rather someone who is already familiar with the program; they will also need an assistant director; I didn't need one because the program wasn't as big as it is now." Victoria said, "Would Valor be a good candidate? Ms. Dorothy said, "Yes, it only requires a high school diploma." Victoria looks puzzled knowing Valor did not have a high school diploma. She then said, "I'll speak with Valor about the position. When valor came into the clinic that afternoon, Victoria mentioned the position to her. Valor said, "I won't be able to do that, I dropped out of school." Victoria said, "Remember what our names stand for." We will help each other. Victoria pulled up some information on How to get your GED and gave it to Valor. Valor said, "What is this?" Victoria said, "I will help you get your GED so you can become my assistant." Valor said, "No one has ever done anything like that for me before." Victoria said, "That's what friends are for."

Later on Victoria's father came home whistling and saying, "God is good". "I have some good news to tell the Family." While eating dinner, her father said, "I have been offered another job that is going to pay me twice as much as the job I have. He went on to say, "Bob and Billy are the owners of the diner we ate at on Saturday; they offered me to be a partner in their business once they are discharged from the hospital." Bob and Billy grew up in a very wealthy family, but they did not present themselves that way. People did not know it until they were much older. Neither of them had wives nor children; they just always wanted to help people. Well the night ended with smiles on everyone faces. Victoria began helping Valor prepare for her GED. She wanted her to be completed around or about the time she graduates; meanwhile Victoria needed to go shopping for a dress for her graduation. Victoria and Valor met at the center and walked to the outlet mall. Victoria tried on several dresses and finally found the perfect dress. Valor told Victoria, "I have some good news; I passed the first part of my GED class." Victoria told Valor how proud of her she was. Valor went on to say, "No one has ever believed in me like you have. Victoria said, "That's what friends do for each other." Today Bob and Billy were discharged from the hospital. Victoria's father went to meet with them so he could familiarize himself with the business. While he was there he mentioned that Victoria was graduating in a few weeks. Bob and Billy said they will be at Victoria's graduation. Bob and Billy became family with Victoria's family. After church on Sunday's, they would eat dinner at each other's homes. Valor began going to church with Victoria also. Victoria told her mother what she was doing to help Valor get her GED. Her mother suggested that she will make Valor a dress for such a great occasion. Victoria was happy with that idea. This week was the week for testing for Victoria; she will be graduating on Friday. Valor has now passed the 2nd part of her GED course. She has one part to go to complete the course and receive her GED. Victoria's father has done so well at his present location that he was offered his own location on the east side of town. All the profits that he makes will be his; it will be his own store. Things are better than they have been before.

Graduation day is here and Victoria is so excited. Victoria has to be at the school one hour before the ceremony. Valor called Victoria's mother to ride with her to the graduation. Valor did not let Victoria know that she was going to attend her graduation because she wanted to surprise her. As they were marching down the field and calling out names the speaker announced there will be a special presentation. Valor stood up and the mistress of ceremony asked Victoria to stand up. Valor said, "I would like you to know you are very special to me and your kindness has taught me to love myself so I can love others; you have stood by me and I appreciate you for that; I also wanted to let you know that I have received my GED." Victoria covered her face as tears streamed down. When she calmed down, she shouted, "I knew you could do it." After graduation everyone went to Victoria's house. Bob and Billy presented Victoria with a $5,000.00 check; she was so shocked because she has never had that much money before. She embraced Bob and Billy with a hug to show her appreciation. Victoria's mother told Valor that she was glad she and Victoria were friends and she wanted to give her something. Victoria's mother pulled out a beautiful Fuchsia and Black dress. Valor eyes teared up and could not believe anyone would do that for her. Meanwhile, Victoria's father came in and gave her a set of keys. She said, "What are these for?" Her father said, "I'm giving you the old car because I bought a new family car." Later that evening Victoria and Valor took a ride in her car; they went to the diner and had a cup of hot chocolate. Weeks had gone by since graduation and Victoria was at the center even more so. Ms. Dorothy asked Victoria to let Valor know she needs to come in and fill out paperwork for the assistant position. When Victoria told Valor the news she was so excited. After weeks of training, Ms. Dorothy decided it was time to retire. She felt Victoria knew her job well enough to handle it. Victoria and Valor decided to give Ms. Dorothy a retirement party. All the people in the program participated. Everyone said nice things about Ms. Dorothy and she was presented with a plaque. Victoria and Valor was in charge of the entire program. Everything was running smooth and more and more people were joining the program. The word had gotten out how successful the program was doing so the owner of the company met with Victoria and Valor. The owner of the company decided to expand the company and put another location on the eastside of town. He nominated Valor to run the center on the eastside. Valor had mixed emotions because she and Victoria had become the best of friends. Valor accepted the job and she moved to the eastside of town. Victoria and Valor met every two weeks for the past month. Victoria and Valor would meet at her father's diner on the eastside of town. Meeting on the eastside would give Victoria a chance to see her father because he has been so busy. This particular day Valor did not seem herself; she was extremely quiet. Victoria asked, "Is anything wrong?" Valor said she was having a few problems with her male friend. She also said he was very controlling and she did not know what to do about it. Victoria asked, "What type of things is he doing?" Valor said, "He doesn't want me to have friends besides him." Victoria told Valor that is a sign of a dangerous person. Valor wanted to know how to get out of the relationship without getting hurt or getting others involved. Meanwhile, while they were talking, Valor's friend walked in. He approached the table and he asked Valor what time was she coming home. Valor told him as soon as she and Victoria get through meeting. Victoria did not like the look on his face or the sound in Valor's voice. It seemed as though she was afraid of him. When Valor's friend left out of the diner; Valor let out a big sigh. Victoria said, "How could you be with someone so controlling?" Valor said, "He says he loves me." Victoria reminded Valor that she must love herself and not look for happiness in someone else." Valor said, "Enough about me, what about you?" Victoria said she will be single until she meet the right person. Victoria also told Valor that she has to demand respect because a person will only do what you allow them to do. Victoria has been going to church on a regular basis. Since Valor moved to the eastside, she hasn't been attending church anywhere. Well, it was getting late, so they said their good-byes and will meet again in a few weeks.

While driving home, Victoria's phone rang and it was her mother. She told Victoria she did not feel well and she needed to go to the hospital. Victoria told her mother to call 911 and she will meet her at the hospital. When Victoria arrived at the hospital, her mother was stabilized on a stretcher. She consulted the physician's regarding her mother's condition. It turns out that she has a blood clot on her lungs. Victoria's eyes watered up for a moment, but then she pulled herself together before calling her father. While her father was in route to the hospital, he began to pray. He said, "Lord I know we haven't been doing everything right, but we are trying; I ask you to keep my wife, but nevertheless let your will be done." When he arrived at the hospital his wife was still stabilized but the doctors wanted to meet with the family. The doctor's said the situation was not looking good and it was nothing more they could do but make her comfortable. As her father began expressing his love to her mother, she grabbed both their hands and said, "It's going to be alright." Victoria asked her mother what she meant by that. Her mother said, "God is in control of everything." The family knew then that she probably would not make it through the night. Her mother overheard Victoria tell her father, "Look like when everything is going well, this happens; I don't understand." Her mother said, "Victoria, God put me in your life for **a reason:** To be your mother and give you guidance; **a season:** To raise you until you can carry yourself; **a lifetime:** Gave me enough time to accept Christ as my savior so I can see you again." Tears streamed down Victoria's face and she said, "I don't know how to let you go." Her mother then said, "God will give you peace." Her father was also crying and told his wife how much he loved her. About that time it was getting hard for her to breath. She grabbed their hands and said, "Take care of each other." She closed her eyes and she died. Victoria and her father held on to each other like never before. When Victoria and her father returned home, she called Valor and told her the news. Valor cried with Victoria and asked if there was anything she could do. Victoria told Valor she will let her know. Everything changed so fast for the family. Victoria and her father began making funeral arrangements. The word got out about Victoria's mother. There were many phones calls and flowers sent to Victoria's home. The family decided not to prolong the funeral, so it they had it within a week. Well the morning of the funeral, Victoria and her father got up and ate breakfast and talked about the good times they shared with her mother. As Victoria and her father arrived at the funeral there were a lot of familiar faces. It made Victoria feels good knowing she had much support from her co-workers, Billy, Bob and Valor was also there. Her father was holding up really well. As the funeral went on, people said some nice things about Victoria's mother. At the end of the service, Victoria's father stood up and thanked everyone for their support. Later that evening Victoria and her father was sitting at home and he said, "I'm glad me and your mother re-dedicated our life to God because I know I wouldn't have been able to handle your mother's death." Victoria told her dad that it was time for them to move and start over; her father agreed. They decided that they will find a home that is not too far from either of their jobs. Her father then said, "It's getting late and I'm kind of tired, it's been a long day;" Victoria agreed.

As she settled down in her room the telephone rang, it was valor crying. Victoria said, "What is wrong?" Valor said, "My boyfriend hit me and out of fear, I picked up a bat and hit him across his back; he is in and out of consciousness." Victoria told Valor to call 911 and that she was on her way. By the time Victoria arrived, the police had already gotten there. The ambulance had already taken her male friend to the hospital. Valor gave a police report and decided she was not going to the hospital. The police told Valor that if she was not going to press charges, they were going to pick them up. The police told Valor that this young man has prior arrest for domestic violence. Valor said she had learned a valuable lesson; always do back ground checks on a person you are not familiar with. A few weeks passed and everything was back to normal. Valor went back to running the center on the east side. The center had become very popular. Each year the centers began to have an annual banquet. Well neither Victoria nor Valor had dates to this upcoming event which was about in two weeks. Valor and Victoria decided to go out to ladies night at this nice club on Thursday night. Victoria called in advance and made reservations for the two of them. Victoria and Valor arrived at the club around the same time. As they walked in, soft music was playing and it was a real cozy atmosphere. Their table was ready and they sat down and while they were enjoying the music, a gentleman approached the table and asked Victoria if she would like to dance; Victoria being a little hesitant said, "Sure." While dancing they introduced themselves and the nice smell of his cologne set the mood. While they continued to dance, another gentleman approached the table where Valor was sitting alone. He asked her to dance, but Valor refused. Then he asked could he join her at the table. Valor nodded her head for him to sit down. Valor said in a very defensive voice, “I’m not interested in getting with anyone; I just got out of an abusive relationship.” He then said, “I’m sorry to hear that, but I saw you here looking very nice and I thought I would ask you for a dance; sorry if I disturbed you." As the gentleman go up to leave, Valor said, “I’m sorry, please sit down; I don’t mean to take my frustrations out on you.” He politely sat down and they began to talk. By that time, Victoria and her gentleman friend came and joined them at the table. They all introduced themselves and began engaging in common conversations. They had been there for a few hours and they both had to work the next day. Victoria and Valor said their good-byes to their gentleman friends and they continued talking. They both agreed that the gentleman were nice; they said their goodnights and went their separate ways.

As Victoria drove home, her cell phone rang; it was the young man she met at the club. He wanted to make sure she was alright and she was making it home alright. He also told her he enjoyed tonight and he would like to see her again; Victoria agreed. When Victoria arrived home she called Valor and made sure she also made it home safely. Victoria mentioned that the young man she met at the club called her; Valor said that her gentleman friend did not call her. Victoria tries to reassure her that maybe he doesn't want to push you, so he may call later. Valor said, "I was a little tough on him when I met him, but I was just angry." Victoria told Valor that they will talk later this week at their meeting. As Victoria laid down in bed she heard a moan; she got up and her father's door was cracked, he was in there mourning the loss of her mother. Victoria never said anything to her father because she knows it takes time to get over such a tragic situation. This was a new day for Victoria and her father; this was the first full day that they had to really face reality without her mother. They both had to re-adjust their schedules because things were already done a certain way when her mother was alive. Victoria decided in her heart that she would do her best to take care of her father. Victoria and her father was very hard workers. Over a period of time they became wealthy and opened a center to help those that were less fortunate. Every Sunday her father fed the homeless at the restaurant. Victoria and Valor kept in touch and remain friends until this day. People will come into our lives and it's all in learning from them or them learning from you. Everything happens for a reason. Every name means something, but the name of Jesus means everything.

5 REAL RELATIONSHIPS

"CAN YOU RELATE"

"This is about 3 women involved in similar relationships that are taking them through many changes. Maria is married with a poor self esteem that deals with **Mental Abuse** from her husband. Mary is single with no self-esteem that deals with **Physical Abuse** from her boyfriend and Meagan is going through a divorce that deals with a husband with **Spousal Abuse**. They end up meeting at one place that changed their lives forever.

Maria is a tall slender person with a nice personality. She is very outspoken, except when it comes to speaking up for herself. She has been married to Bill for 15 years; who works for the railroad company. Mary is very stout and she is a bit shy with a big heart. She is a very hard worker; she is currently working two jobs. She had been dating Aaron for the past five years; he works odd jobs from time to time. Megan is a homemaker and she is going through a divorce after 10 years of marriage; she use to be a school teacher until her husband convinced her to stop working; Jim is the president of a large firm. There were these 3 friends living in a small southern town. They had a population of about 5000 people. These 3 friends have something in common; none of them have kids and are all in relationships. Maria is a 43 years old who is married; Mary is a 40 years old who is single; and Megan is 45 years old who is going through a divorce. Since they all have busy lives, they don't get a chance to see each other that much. They decided to meet for brunch. It would give them time to catch up on old times. They planned to meet at the restaurant called "Happy Eating." Every since Maria, Mary, and Megan made plans for their luncheon, they have been calling each other building up the excitement. One day Megan called Mary to just see if she wanted to go shopping after brunch and then she will call Maria and let her know also. Well, while Meagan was talking to Mary, she heard Aaron in the back ground, "What are you doing home? Mary trying not to show fear in her voice, politely said, "I was off today." He then said, "I need to know when you are off". She abruptly told Megan that she will speak with her later. Soon after hanging up with Mary, Megan called Maria and told her about the situation with Mary. Maria set quietly on the phone, and Megan said, "Are you there? Maria softly said yes. Megan asked, "Is there anything wrong? Maria said, "I can relate to Mary because Bill has been acting really strange lately." He has been starting all types of arguments with me, calling me out of my name, and then he has began drinking, something he doesn't normally do. "Maria said, "I don't know what else to do." Megan then said, "I have not told anyone this, but Jim is asking me to give him a divorce and wants the house. Maria said, "That is not right, he has a good paying job, and you are not working." Megan said, "Well I have really been stressed out over this whole divorce thing. Then Maria said, "Let's call Mary on a three-way. While everyone is on a 3-way, Mary apologizes to Megan about the situation that happened earlier, but they all confessed to each of their relationships and promised they will confide in one another.

The day had finally come for the ladies to have their luncheon. It was a nice and sunny day. Megan arrived at the restaurant first and seen that neither Mary nor Maria had arrived yet, so she got a table and ordered water for everyone. Soon after, Maria arrived and they greeted each other with a hug. Mary called and said she was running a little late. After Mary arrived, they all embraced each other with a hug. Megan said, “Is everyone ready to order”? Both Mary and Maria said, “Yes.” Well, while we were waiting on our food, Megan said to Mary, “Are you going to take off your shades”? Mary softly said, “I can’t.” Megan and Maria looked with deep concern in their faces and said, “Why not”? She said, “Aaron hit me in my eye.” Both Megan and Maria immediately went and embraced Mary. They asked, “How long has this been going on”? Mary said, “For quite sometime, I know I should have told someone, but I did not want to get him in trouble. Megan said, “I understand because I’m going through a situation also.” “My husband Jim has been cheating on me for a while, that is why he is asking for a divorce. Megan went on to say, it started when Jim started coming home late; I would question him about where he was and he would start raising his voice and yelling. I just get quiet so he could be quiet.

One night he told me he had a meeting at his job so I became suspicious and followed him. I followed him to a home where he picked up a young lady. I thought, "It's probably his co-worker and they are meeting with others." Well, it came to an end when we turned into the parking lot of a Hotel. I followed them inside; the lady with him waited in the lounge bar. As they approached the elevators, they kissed each other. I ran out of the hotel in tears and in a rage. I went home and he came a few hours later. I never said anything to him to this day. I have been getting all my information together for my lawyer regarding our divorce. Maria said; "I guess confession is good for the soul." Bill has been very abusive to me." He has been saying things like: "You are good for nothing", "I wish I would have never married you", "You can go back home to your mother." I beg him not to talk me that way, but he continues to do so. Maria, Mary, and Megan made a vow that they will call each other no matter what is going on. They said they will get through this together. They all agreed to try and work out their situations at home.

They decided to ask each gentleman to go the church services with them; they all agreed. All couples met at the 11:00 a.m. services that morning. The minister said, "I have a 3 topic subject; "Love your Wife, Treat her right, and Be Faithful When the pastor gave the name of the topic, Maria's husband Bill began squirming in his seat; Mary's boyfriend Aaron put his head down, and Megan's husband was just in shock. The main thing that got their attention was when the pastor said, "You can't Love your wife if you are not faithful, "You can't treat her right if you are not faithful", and you can't be faithful if you are not faithful." When church services were over, each couple went their separate ways. A few months later, Maria, Mary, and Megan met again at the restaurant; each had good news. Maria said, "Bill has been treating her like a queen and has apologized for his past actions. Bill also has been going with her to church every Sunday; their relationship is better than ever. Mary said, "Aaron has been holding down the same job and has apologized for the way he treated her in the past; he goes to church with her occasionally. Mary is now working one job. Megan said, "She and Jim did get a divorce and he has given her the house and alimony; he just could not forgive himself for cheating on her, but they did remain friends."

Senseless

Cold

Angry

Revengeful

Terrified

Insensitive

Sad

Scared

Unforgiving

Envious

Scar Tissue leaves a mark to remind us of the pain that was once there. These actions are a wall-built up to keep from getting hurt again! On the inside these type of people are very loving and kind, but the scaring is so deep, you will have to get to the root of the problem; the sad thing is that sometimes you never get to the root. When someone scars you it leaves a mark in your flesh. Most Scars come from people that are closest to us.

Living in a world that is ever changing is one thing, but living in a large city sometimes can be a real challenge. The days, months, and years pass by so fast. The bright lights at night make it hard to sleep; horns blowing and people up all night. Jay has learned throughout his life that the city life is not for everyone. Jay grew up in a dysfunctional environment. Jay grew up with his mother but his father was not in his life at all. He did his best not to become a product of his environment. Life can sometimes deal you a rough hand, but you have to deal with the hand you have been dealt; sometimes it's from the scar tissue of others. As usual mom trying to make ends meet by working two jobs; which left Jay fending for himself. They lived in a small neighborhood where people knew each other. As Jay became a teenager, things begin to change. One day as Jay was walking to school, he met an older man that he would often see in passing; his name was Ray. As time went on, they became friends . Jay will never forget it was on a Friday afternoon after leaving school; Ray called him as he was passing by to come to his house. As he approached Ray, he said, "Sit down and talk with me son." Ray began to tell how he grew up back in the days; Ray said he did everything that he thought he could do. At this point, Jay thought that was cool. Jay sit and listened to several of his stories. Jay then said, "It's getting late, I better get home." Ray said, "I have known your mother for a long time." I know she is still at work; I'm cooking dinner and you are welcome to join me if you like. Jay decided to stay and eat dinner. Time went by and it was about time for his mother to get off work. When his mother arrived home, he told her about his visit with Mr. Ray. She said, "I would rather you not go to someone's house without letting me know." Jay said, "Ray said he had known you for a long time." Fay said, I have spoken to him a time or two, but I don't personally know him." Jay's mother began getting some weekends off due to job slowing down. He began to go in town with her on weekends and it was a totally different world out there. The weekends his mother worked, left him home alone. This particular Saturday he decided he to go into town ; he went to the mall where kids his age were hanging out. While sitting in the Mall, a young lady approached him and they exchanged names; she also introduced him to her friends she was hanging out with. Everyone seemed very friendly; they let him know that he can hang out with them whenever he's in town. They had a great time at the mall, but he realized that it was getting late and he had to get home before his mother gets off of work. The bus only passes every 30 minutes; and he had just missed the bus so he had to wait another 30 minutes. He began to get worried because by the time the next bus pass and he gets home, his mother will be there already. The 30 minutes went by and he was on his way home finally. He felt a tap on his shoulder, it was Mr. Ray; was he glad to see him. They rode and talked until they got to their destination. Jay never asked Mr. Ray what he was doing on that side of town. As Jay approached his home, he could see the lights on, so that meant his mother was already home. He was thinking about what excuse he would give her. As he came into the house, he immediately said, "Hi mom"; she said, "Where have you been this late?; "With some friends from school, I know it's late and it won't happen again."

Jay continued going to the mall meeting his friends the weekends his mother was working. Ray noticed that Jay had not been coming around anymore; so this particular day as Jay was walking from school,

Ray called him over to his house. As he walked up, he could see Mr. Ray through the screen door; he was cooking. He said, "Come on in, it's open." Jay was hungry and the food smelled so good. Mr. Ray said," you are welcome to eat dinner if you would like"; Jay agreed. Ray began to tell Jay some old stories about his life again. He told Jay he had done some things that he was ashamed of. He said, "The things I did back then, I would be in jail today"; that left Jay in suspense. Jay could not stop thinking about what Ray meant by that statement. When he got home, his mother was still at work. When his mother arrived from work and he let her settle down, he told her he needed to talk with her. He knows he probably would get scolded for going to Mr. Ray's house, but at this point he was too curious to care. He went on to tell his mother how Ray had secrets and that in this day and time he would have gone to jail for what he done back then. His mother then said, "Jay, everyone has secrets." He said, "What do you mean by that mom?" She began to explain to Jay; "I have not told you a lot of things to protect you, but I believe you are old enough to know." She said, "Me and your father split up long before you were ever born and I have been living here alone." "A terrible thing happened to me years ago while coming home from work; I was attacked from behind and I was beaten and raped and until this day, I still don't know who done this to me." Jay went to his mother and put his arm around her and said, "I'm so sorry this happened to you." "Mom, what do you think Ray is talking about?" She said, "I don't know, are you thinking what I'm thinking?" "Ray says he knows you real well, but you said you don't know him like that; what do you think that mean?" Fay became curious and Jay said he will look into it more by talking with Mr. Ray; meanwhile Fay will contact the Police Department to see if the case can be re-opened.

As time went on there were no leads after contacting the police department. It dawned on Fay that the person that attacked her had to live not far from her; after all back then it was a small community. Jay kept playing Mr. Ray's conversation over in his mind; he came to the conclusion; "What if Ray raped my mother; how will I get him to confess it." Jay did not tell his mother what he was thinking; he decided to take matters into his own hands. Jay knew that he had to pass by Mr. Ray's home every day. This particular day, Mr. Ray called Jay over as he passed by. As they talked as usual; Jay asked, "Ray what happened to you when you said you could go to jail for something?" He said, as he cleared his throat; "I used to date a young lady a long time ago; I was in love with her, but I found out she was not in love with me." Being curious, Jay said, "What happened?" Ray said, "Well, me and this particular young lady went out to the movies and as we walked home from the movies, we were approached by a gang of guys who wanted me to share my girlfriend; I wasn't going to do that so I had to fight all of them." I ended up getting hit in the head with a pipe; woke up in the hospital with a concussion. Until this day I had no contact with that young lady again. I blame myself for not protecting her. Jay said, " If you don't mind telling me, "What was her name?" Her name was Lena. Jay had a sigh of relief because his mom name was Fay. Now Jay will have to start a new search to find this awful person who done this to his mother; so he thought. After a few days went by, he sat down to talk to his mother to let her know about the visit with Mr. Ray. Jay told his mother that Ray said he dated a lady named Lena. His mother said, "What?" She became very nervous and hysterical. She said, "There is something I need to tell you; I changed my name from Lena to Fay after being raped; I was so ashamed that I wanted to start over fresh and leave the past behind." Jay said, "So mom are you saying this is the guy who raped you?" She said, "I believe it is." Jay said," the story Ray told me was; he was approached by several men and he was hit in the head with a pipe and never knew what happened to the young lady." Fay said, "He was a good liar." Jay stood up and said. "I'm going to confront him with this." His mother said, "Don't take the law into your own hands. So now that Fay knows it was Mr. Ray; she then told Jay she had something else to tell him; he said, "Nothing could be worse than this." She said, "I became pregnant as a result of the rape." Jay replied, "Are you telling me he is my father?" Anger rose up in Jay because not only is he torn between the man who raped his mother, but also a man that is his father. Fay wants to report this situation to the police on tomorrow, but not until Jay talk to Ray face to face.

The very next day while walking home from school; Jay went to Ray's house and knocked on the door; as usual he was in there cooking. Ray said, "Come on in son and have a seat." Jay said, "Don't call me son, you lied to me about everything and you raped my mother." Ray said, "What are you talking about I told you the young lady name was Lena and your mother name is Fay." Jay said, "She changed her name due to being raped she was ashamed, angry, terrified, scared and pregnant." Ray said, "Pregnant; so what happened to the child." Jay being so angry said, "He died." Ray just stood there in shock. Jay said," We are turning you over to the police." Mr. Ray began to panic and stumbled onto a chair; he said, " I knew this would be the death of me; all these years I have been worrying when the day would come and I be uncovered; it was a senseless, cold thing that I have done and I don't blame you for retaliating; I was young and stupid." Ray went on to say, "I'm sorry for ruining you and your mother's life. Jay said, "You know I can kill you and no one would know it. Ray said, 'I'm probably better off dead." He went on to say, " I didn't have parents to love me, so I tried to make Lena love me. Jay said, "You can't make anyone love you, they must choose to love you." Ray crying hysterically as if he was hyperventilating; it scared Jay so he rushed over to console him. He sat Ray up so he can get some air. Mr. Ray said," How could you help me after all I have done?" Jay said, because I'm your son." Ray said, "I thought, you said the child died." Jay said, "I wanted to die after I found out what you done to my mother, but I would just be repeating the same thing she done." Jay thought about what his mother said, and decided not to take matters into his own hands. He made sure Ray was ok before leaving and told him he will have to think about turning him over to the authorities. Ray said, "One way or the other I will be alright."

So much has happened in the past few days that Jay decided that he needed to clear his head and stop communicating with Ray for a while. A few days passed by Jay had been noticing that Ray had not been sitting outside nor having his door opened. Jay decided to go by to make sure Ray was alright. He thought about the last comment Ray said before he left. He walked up to the door and knocked, but no one answered. He went around to the side and looked through the window; he saw Ray lying on sofa with arm hanging off; he knocked on window, but no answer or no movement of Mr. Ray. Jay broke the window to get in. When inside, he rushed over to Mr. Ray; he was not breathing; he saw an alcohol bottle on the floor. He immediately turned him over and began to minister CPR (Christ Preparing Restoration). As he was ministering, being afraid his dad would die, he began to pray. He told his Dad that he loved him regardless of his past; he knows the thing he has done has scared so many people, but he is willing to forgive him. Immediately when he said the word forgive, his father began coughing and revived. Ray said in a whispering, "How could you forgive me after all that I have done?' Jay said, "When I forgive you it releases me to love; and I want you to forgive yourself." For the first time, Ray and Jay hugged with compassion; like a father hugs his children. For the first time Ray really felt how it feels to be loved. Things began to change for Ray and Jay; they began to build a father son relationship.

As time went on, Jay would stop by his father's house everyday after school to check on him. Jay's mother was a little bitter because she did not expect this type of relationship to develop between Ray and Jay. She is still dealing with scars from the past and can't seem to move on. She began to resent the relationship between Ray and Jay. She wants Ray to pay for what he has done, but Jay has found in his heart to forgive Ray. Fay being so bitter for so many years that forgiveness is the farthest thing from her mind. Jay and his mother's relationship became very distant since he and his father became closer. Fay had mixed feelings about the entire situation. She is glad Jay knows that Ray is his father and she is torn between the two. Fay decided to hold off on contacting the police for now. It was coming up to the holidays; this has never been a good time for Fay because it always made her feel lonely. Fay asked to work over-time at the restaurant to make some extra money. This is definitely going to be a different holiday for the first time. As time went on Fay began neglecting herself and not taking care of herself like she normally does. She could not get over the fact that this man is still walking the streets after all these years; she wanted him to pay, but now she doesn't want to take her son away from his father. Fay began to start feeling bad on and off. She thought it was from working so much. She began to cough really badly and her body was very achy. She refuses to go the doctor. Due to being sick so much she had to cut back on her hours. Everyday Jay would stop by his father's house after school to check on him. Well this particular day he and his father got on the conversation of his mother. Ray mentioned to Jay that he wished somehow that Fay would forgive him. He knew that he could not make it right but he just wanted to be at peace about the situation. Jay told his father to just pray about it.

When Jay arrived home after leaving his father's house, he walked in to the house and it was very dark. He called out to his mother, but there was no answer. He started walking towards her bedroom when he discovered her on the floor. He immediately went to her and she was barely breathing. He immediately called 911 and then called his father. His father rushed over to assist Jay with his mother. When Fay came through, she saw ray, and immediately said, "I want him out of here." Ray said, "I know you hate me, but I'm only trying to help." Fay said, "I don't need your help." As Ray got up to leave the ambulance had arrived. The paramedics came inside to get Fay stabilized . They encouraged Fay to see her primary care physician as soon as possible. When the paramedics got Fay stabilized they left. Fay overheard Ray tell Jay, "I will have to live with this for the rest of my life; there is no sign of forgiveness from your mother." Ray and Jay got together and made the appointment for Fay to see her primary care doctor. Fay's appointment will be on tomorrow at 4:00 p.m. Due to Fay being so weak, Ray was the person that would have to take her, but she did not know that at the time. The appointment was set for school after hours because Jay knew that Fay would not let Ray near her. The next day when Jay came from school he immediately rushed home to help his mother get ready for her doctor's appointment. She asked Jay, "Have you called the cab yet?" Jay hesitated and said, "Mom, we are not taking a cab, Ray is taking us." Fay could barely talk, she said, "He is not taking me anywhere." Jay said, "I will be there and I promise I will not let anything happen to you." That is the only way Fay got into the vehicle with Mr. Ray. When Fay's name was called, Jay went to the back with his mother to see the physician. They ran all types of test and x-rays but could not find anything wrong. The doctor said maybe if things don't get better they will order a stress test. The Doctor gave Fay a few days off to get her strength back before returning to work. One day while Fay was at work, her boss noticed that she has been limping and in a lot of pain. He went to her, but she said she was alright. Weeks passed and Fay seemed as though she was getting worse again. She decided to take a leave of absence. As Fay sat in deep thought, she remembered what she overheard Ray telling Jay about forgiveness. She was curious so she decided to research about forgiving.

There were a few months left in school and Jay had to finish school but his mother had become very ill. There was no one left to care for her but Ray. Jay had to figure out how he was going to tell his mother. It was stressing him out so one day while he and his mother were sitting around talking he blurted out that Ray would have to see about her while he was at school. Fay said, "I rather die if I have to let Ray take care of me." Fay does not want to let go of the hurt and pain because it is so deeply rooted within her. Fay doesn't realize that she must forgive Ray in order to get well. See the problem was in her mind even though this physically happened to her. She did not know how to let it go. When you harden your heart for someone one and you want them to pay for what they have done it will make you sick. As she continued to do her research on forgiveness it was convicting her. She fought it with everything she had in her because she refused to forgive someone that done such a thing to her. One day while home alone, Fay accidently fell and twisted her ankle. She scooted herself over enough to reach the phone. It took everything in her to call Ray, but he was the closet one and the only one she really knew even though she did not trust him. She called and when Ray picked the phone up, as she cleared her throat, she said, “Ray it’s me, Fay; "I have fallen and I need your help." Ray immediately hung up the phone and rushed over to help Fay. You can never say who you will not need in the time of trouble. Even though Fay felt Ray has done her a great injustice she doesn’t realize she has done someone wrong herself. After Ray helped Fay get stabilized, he headed to the door to leave. Fay said, “Ray thank you, but that don’t mean I forgive you.” Ray said, “I know I can’t repay what I have done to you years ago, but if you just give me a chance to show you I have changed.” Since that day, Ray would go by every day and check on Fay. In order to remove scar tissue Fay had to go through surgery. During surgery you will need all kinds of sharp objects. A knife is used which is the word of God (Cuts like a two-edged sword). Fay has to allow the word of God to work on her to ease the pain. The biggest pain of the surgery was seeing Ray’s face every day. If the pain remained the same after seeing Ray that let Fay know that something was still wrong and she needed more time for the wound to heal. The pain will ease when you start applying the word of God to life’s situations. The problem was caused from harboring unforgiveness. In order for Fay to receive her total healing, she has to forgive Ray. Fay wanted Ray to suffer until she felt he paid for what he had done to her. She has to come to the realization that she has a right to press charges, but realizes that the case is very old and wonders if it is really worth all the energy and effort that will be put into getting Ray convicted after all these years. She wondered if the pain will go away once he is convicted or is it out of revenge. If Ray goes to jail, then Jay will miss out on the time that he has trying to build a father/son relationship. All these things went through Fay's mind. As time went on Fay's condition worsened. She could not understand it because she followed all the doctor's orders. Spiritually, she was listening to the wrong doctor. In life we have to face our problems head on to get through them. Sometimes we want to go around the storms of life because going through it causes too much pain. Fay did not realize the seeing Ray everyday would eventually make it easier to deal with her past. As Fay began to read the bible on a daily basis; she started to see her pain subside, but she noticed when Ray came around she would get bitter again. The spirit of God spoke to Fay and told her not to just read the word but apply it to her life. Finally, the light came on; she realized that she would not get over her past if she did not try to let it go. Fay made up in her mind that no matter how bad it hurts, she will start trying to mend the fences with Ray and her past. Normally, Ray would come by and check on Fay every day, but this particular day he did not come by. Fay found that to be very strange. Fay picked up the phone and called Ray, but there was no answer. Fay realized that something was wrong. With Jay being at school, Fay knew she was too weak to go check on Ray. Now she really began to worry. She also did not realize that the word of God was working on her hardened heart. The day went on and Jay finally arrived home from school. Fay immediately said, "Ray did not come today." Jay said, "Why?" Fay explained that she tried calling, but there was no answer. Jay immediately ran out of the house to go to check on Ray. As he got closer he could see people standing in the street in front of Ray's home. As he arrived at the door, he could see the paramedics working on Ray. It was told to Jay that Ray had a heart attack. When Jay let the paramedics know that he was Ray's son, they let him inside. Once Ray was stabilized he told Jay to tell Fay that he was sorry for not being there for her. Jay was torn between his mother and father seeing that both of them needed him. He could not go with his father to the hospital due to his mother being ill. As he walked home, he was contemplating on how he was going to tell his mother being that she hated Ray, so he thought. He also thought to himself, "Why tell her, she doesn't care anyway." When Jay walked into the house, he looked a little down. Fay hysterically said, "Well, where is Ray? Did you see him?" Jay said, "Ray had a heart attack and told me to tell you that he is sorry that he could not be here for you". Fay became teary-eyed and said, "Oh that's alright, he must take care of himself." Jay was surprised at the answer his mother gave. Fay told Jay she has been reading her bible and it's helping her to soften her heart towards Ray. She said, "maybe Ray had a heart attack from me being so hard on him. Jay said, "Mom, you are too hard on yourself. Fay said, "No if I would have just forgiven him this may not have happened."

The light came on, she said, "It's forgiveness. Jay said, "What are you talking about?" She said, "I have to forgive Ray." With Ray being in the hospital, Fay was trying to figure out a way to tell him. All through the night Fay tossed and turned being anxious to tell Ray the news. Around 9 a.m. Fay called the hospital and was connected to Ray's room. Ray being groggy from the meds answered the phone. Once he heard it was Fay's voice, he said, "I know you hate me, but I can't forgive myself for the wrong that I have done to you." Fay said, "That is what I'm calling to tell you that I forgive you." When Ray heard this, he began to cry. He said, "You don't know how long I have waited to hear those words." Fay said, "I wanted you to pay for what you have done to me, but I realize that I have done someone wrong myself; it may not have been to the extent that you have done, but wrong is wrong." Fay realized that forgiveness not only releases the other person, but releases her to love and move forward in her life. A few weeks passed and Ray was getting released from the hospital. Fay decided that she and Jay would pick Ray up from the hospital. A few days had gone by and Fay realized that she wasn't feeling sick or anything; her focus was not on herself but on someone else. The tables have turned, now Fay is taking care of Ray. See when God does something we can only imagine. Fay never thought she would ever find herself taking care of someone who wronged her in such a way. Without having the God kind of love, you cannot truly forgive. When God gives us something it's of his kind. Everything operates off of love. Fay may have felt she was dealt a bad hand in life; but with God all things are possible. How much do you love? Do you love God enough to accept his Son Jesus? Love can melt the hardest of hearts. Forgiveness doesn't mean you forget, it means you are moving on. What types of scars have people left in your life? Love mixed with forgiveness will remove the pain/scars others leave behind. When are you going to take the bandages off the wounds that other left behind and start healing? Wounds covered cannot heal.

7 When You Think You Know People!

Be careful who you point your finger at!

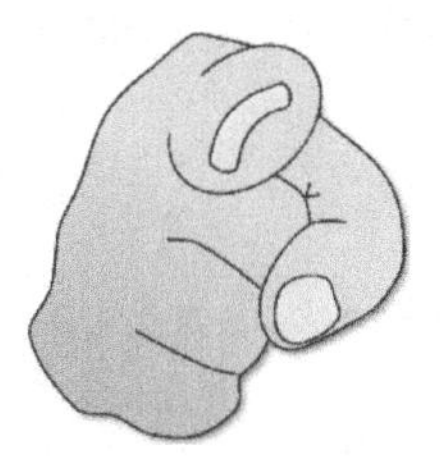

Donna was the type of person that would help anyone. She was put into a situation by one of her church members. Tonya was a new member at the church who had a great number of medical conditions. Tonya kind of used her medical condition to get sympathy from others at times. Tonya has not always been the way she is now, but neither has Donna. As they get to know each other, they will soon find out they are not so different after all.

Sometimes we allow people to put us in awkward situations. Due to a medical condition of one of the church members; Donna was introduced to a lady named Tonya. Tonya was going through a physical dilemma .There was a situation that took place that caused Donna and Tonya to become acquaintances. They really didn't know each other that well, they met through church members who said that Donna was a nice person and she wouldn't mind helping Tonya out. Well, Donna began taking Tonya to all her doctor's appointments and as the days, weeks, and months went by they began to form a friendship. I have learned that just because a person goes to church does not make them a Christian and just because they don't attend church does not mean they are not a Christian. Tonya could not attend church like she wanted to due to her medical condition. Tonya was a middle aged woman around 55, and she had two grown children. Donna was around 50 years old with one child. Seems as though Tonya's children should be doing more for her. One Saturday morning , Tonya called Donna to take her to the grocery store. Being the person Donna was she said, "I'll be there shortly." While in route to Tonya, Donna drove a few blocks, she seen a young lady standing on the corner. Once she stopped at the corner, the young lady approached the car. The lady asked, "Ms. do you have some change to spare." Donna reached into her purse and gave the young lady $5. The young lady said, "Thank you" and walked away. As Donna arrived at Tonya she was already waiting outside. Donna said, " I would have been here sooner, but a young lady that was on the corner stopped me for some change." Tonya knew that was her daughter but never said a word.

On the way to the grocery store, they saw the same lady, but she was getting into a car with a young man. Donna said, "That is the young lady I just gave some money to." Donna did not find it strange for Tonya not to respond because she wasn't a big talker anyway. While in the grocery store and it being such a small community, Tonya ran into her neighbor Mr. Leonard; he is the acting police in the neighborhood. Mr. Leonard said, "every time I pass that corner, I try and give your daughter a word of encouragement. Tonya quickly said, "It was nice seeing you Leonard." Donna eyes lit up and she said, "Did he say your daughter?" Tonya said, "No, I think he may of said my cousin." Donna did not say anything, but she know what she heard. While taking Tonya home, they noticed that the young lady was not on the corner. Well as they pulled up to Tonya' s home, Donna noticed someone looking out of window with the curtains pulled back; when she noticed me looking, she quickly closed the curtains. Donna mentioned to Tonya that she thought she seen someone looking out her window. Tonya said, "No I'm home alone." Donna thought to herself, "Now that is the second time that Tonya lied about something today." As Donna got out the car to help Tonya take her groceries in; Tonya said," Just put them on the steps and I will get them into the house." As Donna drove off, she looked through her mirror and the young lady was in the window again; she also noticed Tonya looking back. When Donna got home and relaxed for the night, she called her friend Alice. She told Alice what had happened and Alice said, "Be careful because if a person can lie to you, it's no telling what else they will do to you." Well the next morning Donna picked Tonya up for church. Donna noticed Tonya looked very tired. Donna said, "Are you alright?" Tonya said, "Yes, just had a long night." Tonya then asked Donna, "How do you go to God and ask him for forgiveness? Donna said, "Just go to God with a sincere heart." Church services went on as usual. After service Alice approached Donna and asked, "What did you find out?" Donna nodded her head to let Alice know that this was Tonya. Alice quickly said, "About our class reunion." Tonya did not seem suspicious at the time.

As Donna pulled up at Tonya's home after church services, Tonya said, "Would you like to come in for some lunch?" Donna being suspicious of everything else said, "Sure." Tonya knew her daughter was not home that time of the day. As soon as Tonya and Donna sat down to eat, there was a knock at the door. It was Mr. Leonard and he told Tonya, "It's your daughter, she has been hit by a car and left for dead." Donna and Tonya immediately got into the car and followed Mr. Leonard down to the scene of the accident. There laid Tonya's daughter and the paramedics working on her to save her life. Tears began to roll down Tonya's face as she was praying under her breath. As Donna and Tonya got closer to the paramedics, Donna said, "That is the young lady I gave money to on yesterday." Tonya said, "Donna I'm so sorry." Donna was hurt because Tonya lied about her daughter. Donna told Tonya she had to leave and have Mr. Leonard take her home. Donna drove up to her home and just sat in the car. She could not believe that Tonya lied to her after all she has done for her. When she entered the house, she heard some noise coming from the back; it was her son. She said, "Son why do you have your vehicle parked in the back of the house?" He said, he was changing a part on it." Donna never thought anything more of it, and went back into the house. She could not wait to call Alice and tell her the news. While talking to Alice, the news came on and Alice said," There was a hit and run today and a young lady was left for dead." Donna said, "Yeah, I was about to tell you that was Tonya's daughter." Alice was shocked to hear that. Donna went on to say; "She was prostituting." Alice said, " I did not know that Tonya had kids around here." Donna said, "I have caught Tonya in several lies since I have been taking her places. " She knew all along that was her daughter when I mentioned it earlier on yesterday and she never said anything; "You can't trust anybody these days."

Well, about that time the news was mentioning a description of the vehicle. Alice said, "Don't your son have a blue truck?" Donna said, "Yes, are you trying to say my son hit Tonya's daughter?" Alice said, "I was just asking because they said it was a black male in a blue truck." Donna began thinking when she came home and her son had his truck in the back yard. She abruptly told Alice that she will call her later. As she went back to speak with her son, he just finish putting a bumper on the front of his truck. Donna said, "Son, did you hear about the hit and run today?" He said nervously, "Oh yeah, that was a terrible thing that happened." She said, "Son is there something you need to tell me?" Her son broke down and cried; he said, "Mama it was an accident." He told her how it happened and she said, "We have to call the police." He said,

"Mama please don't, we can work this out somehow." Donna thought about it and decided not to call the police. Donna told her son that they have to keep it between them. Donna found herself in the same position that Tonya was in; but how was she going to get away with this. A few days had gone by and Donna refused to answer Tonya's phone calls. Well, Tonya decided to ask Mr. Leonard to take her to Donnas' house because she thought maybe something was wrong. As they pulled up, Donnas' car was there and Tonya noticed a vehicle was covered up in the backyard. As Tonya began to get out the vehicle, Donna looked out of her window and immediately came outside. She said nervously, "Hi Tonya, what are you doing here?" Tonya said, "I have been calling you, and since you haven't answered any of my calls, I thought something was wrong." Donna said, "No I have been fine, I just been a little under the weather. Tonya found that strange because Donna did not look or sound ill. Tonya told Donna she will call her later and check on her. As Tonya and Mr. Leonard pulled off, they noticed that part of the vehicle was sticking out. Tonya said, "Wasn't the hit and run vehicle a blue truck?" Mr. Leonard said, "Yes, and it was a black male driving the truck." Tonya said, "You don't think Donnas' son was involved in this do you?" Leonard said, "No she would not keep anything like this from you." Tonya said, “I don't know, I did lie to her about my daughter." Leonard said, "Maybe you should talk to her about what you saw at her house." Tonya said, when I know my child is alright, I will." Tonya had Leonard to take her to the hospital to see her daughter. She was in ICU and could only have limited visits. When Tonya entered the room, it’s like her daughter knew she was there. She immediately said, "Mama, I'm so sorry for putting you through so much." Tonya said, “Did you see the man that hit you?" She said, "All I know he was a black guy with a scar under his left eye." Tonya said, “I just stopped by to check on you, get some rest and I will see you soon." Tonya thought to herself, I have to find a way to see what Donnas' son looks like.

The week was coming to an end and church was on Sunday. Well Saturday night, Tonya called to see if Donna was feeling well enough to pick her up for church. When Donna picked up the phone, she sounded a little sluggish. Tonya said, "Donna, are you alright"? Donna said, "I'm fine." I wanted to know if you will be picking me up for church on tomorrow. Donna said, "I'll be there around 8:00 a.m. As they hung up, Donna did not quite put the phone on the hook. As Tonya went to hang up, she heard some voices on the phone. She put the phone back to her ear and listened. Donnas' voice was very loud and disoriented like a drunken person. This went on for about 15 minutes. When Donna realized that the phone was off the hook, she picked up the phone and said, "Hello", but Tonya did not say anything. She hung up the phone and said to herself; "I wonder if Tonya was listening on the other line?" Well, the next day, 8:00 a.m. came and went. Donna never showed up to pick Tonya up for Church. Tonya called, but no one answered. As the day went on, about 12:30 p.m. Donna pulled in Tonya's driveway. Tonya heard a car outside and went to the door; Donna was coming up the steps. When Donna saw Tonya, she immediately began to apologize about not picking her up for church. Tonya just played it off and said, "It's ok, I know you weren't feeling well the other day." Tonya and Donna sat out on the porch and began to talk. Donna asked Tonya was her daughter out of the hospital; Tonya said, "No she will be getting out later this week.

As they sat around talking, Tonya began to ask Donna about her family. Tonya said, "Donna, I really only know you through acquaintances at church, but we have not really gotten to know that much about each other." Donna began to tell Tonya that she had 1 son and how she raised him by herself after his father left when he was only two years old. She was telling her how hard they had it, but they made it through the tough times. Tonya starting talking about her daughter and how she wishes they would find the person that done this horrible thing. Donna tried to stay as calm as possible without getting fidgety. She abruptly said, "I hope they do to, the person probably was scared and just drove off." All of a sudden there was a silence in the air. Donna said, "I guess I will be going, I have a few errands to take care of today." As she started walking off, Tonya reached and hugged Donna and told her she glad she stopped by. As Tonya hugged her, she could feel Donnas' heart racing really fast, which meant Donna was uneasy about something. They said their good-byes; Donna got into her car and Tonya went into the house. As Donna drove home, she called her son and let him know that this situation is eating her up inside. She told her son that last night she thought she hung up the phone, but realized that it was off the hook and she did not know if Tonya heard her talking to him. He said, "Did she mention it while you were there? Donna said, "No.", he said, "then you don't have anything to worry about."

A few weeks went by and Donna and Tonya were on their way from church when they stopped at a red light. There was this guy who was jay walking across the street; he had dreads and a nice size scar under his left eye. Tonya immediately panicked and said, "That's the guy who hit my daughter." Tonya began getting out the car when Donna reach and grabbed her. Donna said, "What makes you think that is the guy?" She said, "he has a scar under is left eye." Donna said, "But he is walking, not driving." Tonya stopped and said, "Your right; I just want the police to find who did this to my daughter." Donna got flustered and decided to take Tonya home to get some rest." Once Donna brought Tonya home, she rushed home and told her son, Tonya will know it's you if she sees you because she said the person had a scar under his left eye. Donna said," Whatever you do, you must never meet Tonya." Donnas' son agreed to stay out of sight. Donna lived at least 5 miles from Tonya. The neighborhood that Donna lived in was fairly large, but the neighborhood that Tonya lived in was fairly small. More than likely these two neighborhoods; people were unfamiliar with each; so you thought. Tonya kept in touch with Leonard to see if he had come up with any breaks in this case. Leonard could not give her anything without any good leads. Tonya told Leonard about the incident she and Donna had the other day. Leonard said they may have to do something different in order to get some leads. He asked Tonya if she had any suggestions; she said," Maybe we need to have a night of getting to know your neighbors." She said she will also ask Donna to do the same in her neighborhood. Tonya would like the police department to put out posters with a description and a reward that leads to the arrest of the person who committed this act. Wednesday's are bible study at church so Tonya decided that she will approach Donna with the situation on the way to church. While in route to church, Tonya told Donna she and Leonard came up with a way to get leads in her daughter's case and wondered if Donna would like to help them? Donna said, "What is it that I have to do?" Tonya explained that they would have a night out to meet neighbors and put out posters with a description of the gentlemen they are looking for. Donna swallowed real deep, and said, "I will have to get back with you on that." Tonya agreed with Donna and told her not to feel pressured about it. After church was over, Donna asked Tonya, if she mind her stopping to the store before taking her home. Tonya said, "No, I have to get a few items myself." While they were in the store, Donnas' phone rang, it was her son. By then, Tonya had gone over to the next aisle. As Tonya, came back to ask Donna a question, she overheard Donna talking on the phone in a whispering voice; Tonya found that very suspicious. Donna told her son in an undertone voice, "I can't do this anymore." Tonya came around the corner and Donna cleared her throat and said, "I'll talk to you later." Tonya said, "Donna is something wrong, Donna said, "No, you know how your children can be." Tonya said, " I understand. As they walked out the store, Donna told Tonya she forgot to get something in the store, so she sent Tonya to the car. Donna went back to the counter to get a bottle of wine. She had the cashier to make sure she put the wine in two bags. Tonya found it strange after all that time they were in the store, Donna forgot something; Tonya waited for Donna in the car. Tonya felt that something has been going on with Donna since the night she called her. The reason Tonya never mentioned about the phone, she could not understand what Donna was saying; it seemed muffled and far away, but she was talking someone that was in the house with her at the time.

After a few weeks had passed, Tonya called Donna and asked was she going to participate in the neighborhood night out. To keep Tonya from getting suspicious, Donna agreed to do it. The night out would be next weekend. Meanwhile, Tonya's daughter was still recovering from her injuries; she will start taking therapy this week. She will also go to see a psychiatrist to talk about the impact that this has made on her life. She had been having nightmares and not being getting good rest. Few days before the neighborhood watch, Leonard went to Donna and

Tonya's house to give them the flyers to pass out. Well, Leonard decided to go to Donna house first to drop off the flyers. Leonard knocked on the door, no one answered. He left a note with the flyers and put them in the mailbox. As he left; he saw in his rearview mirror a gentlemen going to get the flyers out of the mailbox. Leonard thought nothing of it at the time. When Leonard arrived at Tonya's house to take her flyers, he mentioned the incident that happened at Donnas' house. Tonya told Leonard that Donna has been acting strange lately. Leonard asked, "Does Donna have a son?" Tonya said, "Yes, Donna has a son whom I have never met." Leonard said, "Maybe I need to work at Donnas' neighborhood night and meet some of those people since we are all familiar here." Well the night has come for the watch; look like everything was going good. Everyone was meeting and greeting when Leonard showed up. He saw Donna from a distance and a gentlemen next to her, but as he got closer, the gentlemen looked his way and said something to Donna and starting walking back towards the house. When Leonard walked up, Donna immediately said, "If you would have gotten here a few minutes earlier, you could have met my son." Leonard said, "Maybe one day I will meet him." As the night went on it began to thunder and lighting. Well, everyone was kind of on edge due to the weather. Leonard and Donna stood about to say their good-byes when it started raining. They started running towards Donnas' house since it was closer then Leonard's car. Leonard said, "Is it alright if I stay here until it slack up a bit?" Donna said, "That will be fine." When they walked into the house it was very dark and barely lit up. Donna turned on some lights and offered Leonard to have a seat. She left to go to the laundry room to get a towel so Leonard could dry off. While she was in the other side, her son came into the living room not knowing Leonard was there. As he walked in, he kind of startled Leonard. As they made eye contact, the first thing Leonard noticed was the scar under his eye. They shook hands and introduced themselves. When Donna returned to the room, she was startled to see her son there. All she could think about is that Leonard knows Tonya and he may go back and say something to her about her son. Donna had to find a way to get her son out of the room with Leonard.

Leonard and Donnas' son struck up a conversation. Donna seemed a litter nervous so she immediately said, "Son could you go tend to the laundry in the dryer for me?" He immediately got up and went to the laundry room. Well, a few minutes later, Donna said, "Excuse me Leonard; I have to make sure he gets all the laundry." Leonard just looked, but found it strange that Donna seemed a little over protective of her son. When Donna got to the laundry room, she said, “I don't want you talking to Mr. Leonard he knows Tonya, the lady's daughter that you accidently hit. As Donna went back into the living room, Leonard said, "Seem as though the rain has slacked up, I will be leaving now." Donna walked him to the door and closed it behind him. When Leonard made it to his car, he immediately called Tonya to let her know that he had met Donnas' son and the surprising discovery. After Leonard told this to Tonya, she was very disturbed because this was something very serious and she know that she would have to make a police report. Tonya told Leonard that she would need a few days to get herself together, but she was definitely was going to go to the police station. Tonya called Donna, and she sounded kind of out of it like the last time they spoke. Donna let Tonya know that she was not going to bible study for a while she is dealing with something right now. Tonya asked was there anything she could do; Donna said," No." Tonya knew then that she had to do something right away to get the person that hit her daughter. Early Monday morning Tonya went to visit her daughter and let her know that she will have to report to make a police report.

Tonya's daughter said, "Mom who could have done such a terrible thing?" Tonya said, "We kind of have an idea who may have done this." Tonya let her daughter know that when you get well enough, they will go down to the police station and look at a line up. Finally after another week in the hospital, Tonya's daughter was released to go home. It would be a while before Tonya's daughter make a full recover. Anyway, the next week Tonya and her daughter went go down to the police department and filed a report. Early Sunday morning Donna called to see if Tonya was going to church since her daughter was home from the hospital. Tonya decided to go and asked if her daughter could go because she wanted prayer. Donna said surprisingly, "Sure". This will be Donnas' first time personally meeting Tonya's daughter. As Donna approached Tonya's house she had to calm herself down so she would not become nervous when she see's Tonya's daughter. When she drove into the driveway, Tonya and her daughter was coming out of the house. Donna opened the door for her daughter to sit in the back. As they drove to the church; Donna could not help but stare at Tonya's daughter. At one point her eyes got real watery like she wanted to cry. Tonya looked at Donna and said, "Is something wrong?" Donna said, "No I just was thinking about your daughter and her situation." Tonya told Donna her daughter is filing a police report on Monday, because she remembers that the guy driving the truck has a scar under his left eye. Donna knows that Tonya has never met her son but Leonard have. Donna swallowed deeply, she then said, "How could she know that?" Tonya's daughter mentioned that the person that hit her came to see if she was still breathing and she got a chance to look at him; and remembered a scar under his left eye. After he saw she was breathing, he immediately jumped in his vehicle and sped off.

Church services was going very well so Tonya's daughter went up for prayer. After church service were over Donna brought Tonya and her daughter home. Tonya asked Donna did she want to come in for some lunch, but Donna said "No." Donna could not wait to get home to let her son know that Tonya's daughter is going to the police. Donna began crying and her son said, "Mom don't worry I won't let you take the fall for this." Donna said, "Son what are we going to do?" He said, "We will do like we have always done, leave and go somewhere else". Donna said, "We must pack so we can go because Tonya's daughter is going to the police in the morning". It was getting late, so Donna decided that they would leave early in the morning. The next morning came and instead of them leaving early, they overslept. By that time the door bell rang; it was Leonard, Tonya's friend the police officer. He told Donna that she will need to bring her son down to the station to do a line up. He told her it was just a precaution due to they were looking for a black male with a scar under his left eye. He also told Donna they had at least a number of guys with scars. Donna felt relieved because Tonya's daughter could mistakenly pick out one of the other guys in the line up. After Leonard left, Donna explained to her son that he will have to go down to the station. He said, "I can't go down there; she will identify me." Donna explained that there were several other guys with a scar also. Donna and her son had to be at the station for 1:00 p.m. While they drove down toward the station, her son was nervously tapping on the dashboard. Donna said, “Would you please stop, you are making me nervous." Her son replied, “I can't go back to jail." As they stopped at the red light, Donnas' son jumped out the car and started running the opposite direction." Donna pulled over to the side and the road and go out of the vehicle and yelled, "Son, please stop, everything will be alright"; but he kept running. Donna had no choice but to go to the police station. When Donna arrived at the police station and spoke with the officer ; she explained that her son jumped out of the car and ran the opposite direction. She explained that she tried to stop him. The police department immediately put an alert out on her son.

About an hour had gone by and no sign of her son. The officer told Donna that she will be held until they bring her son in. The officer let her know by him running is a sign of guilt and her being his mother may have already known about this situation, but did not report it. Well, the officer brought Tonya and her daughter out from line up room; when they saw each other; Tonya said, "Donna what brings you here." Donna began telling Tonya the story about her son, "Tonya, said, "Your son hit my daughter and left her for dead and you did not say anything?" Donna said, "I'm sorry, but I was so scared." Tonya and her daughter abruptly left out of the station. Tonya was so upset she sped out of the parking lot; she was driving faster then normal. Her daughter immediately said, "Mom, could you please slow down, you are frightening me." Tonya came to herself and slowed the car down. As they pulled to the red light, there was a gentlemen sitting on a bench as if he was waiting for the bus. When he looked up, he and Tonya's daughter made eye contact and she immediately said, "That's him, the guy that hit me." The guy immediately got up and starting running again, this time Tonya went after him. The gentlemen ran a few blocks and end in a dead end alley. There was no way for him to get out; so Tonya and her daughter got out of the car. Tonya asked him, "Why did you leave my daughter for dead?" He said, "I was scared and did not know what to do." She also told him that his mother was at the police station and they will not release her until he turns himself in. He said, "I can't go back to jail; it was an accident." Tonya said, "Just let me drive you to the station and you could explain your story." After about 30 minutes, Tonya finally talked him into going to the station. While they were in route, he kept apologizing about what happened. Tonya's daughter said, " I forgive you." When she said that tears began to roll down his face. Well they turned into the station; and as Tonya put the car in park; she looked back at Donnas' son and said, I'm sorry it had to end this way." They began walking to the building and Donnas' son stopped and said, "I can't." Tonya's daughter went inside to get an officer while Tonya stayed outside to try and talk him into turning himself in.

When the officer came on the scene; he had his weapon drawn. He said, "Son let's not make this harder than it has to be." He wanted to see his mother to make sure she was alright. The officer brought Donna out to reassure him his mother was alright. Donna said, "Son just turn yourself in and we can get a lawyer to help us." He said, "Mom I can't do this;" and he began walking backwards. The police office said, "Stop or I will shoot"; He said, "Shoot me; If I go back to jail I'm dead already." As long as he had his face to the officer and walking away, the officer did not shoot. As he turned around to begin running a car struck him and he went into the air about 10 feet and landed on his back. Donna rushed over crying and held her son; he was barely breathing. The officer called 911. When the paramedics arrived they immediately began working to get him stabilized, but the trauma to his head was too severe; Donnas' son did not make it. Donna could not believe this was happening. Tonya rushed over and put her hand on Donnas' shoulder and said, "I'm so sorry about this." Donna said my son left your daughter for dead, but now my son is dead." After all was done; Donna had to serve 1000 hours of community service for withholding evidence. Donna felt that this was her fault, because if she would have done the right thing; this could have been avoided. Donna was never the same since this happened. As time went on Donna and Tonya remained friends due to this situation. Tonya's daughter made a full recovery and made a drastic change in her life. Tonya and her daughter now have a stronger relationship than ever. Sometimes life takes us on different roads, but throughout life, when we think we know people; sometimes we really don't.

8

TRUE LOVE BIRDS

Theme: Opposites Attract

"Never judge the outer appearance; judge the heart!

This is about a very beautiful girl named Janice. She met a nice gentleman they fell in love and got married. Her best friend Stacey in the beginning was very happy for her, but as things were continuing to happen for Janice she became jealous of her. Stacey had a past that she kept hidden. Janice judged Teddy by his out appearance, but he was good for her. She judged Stacey by her inner appearance and she was not good for her. Never judge a person by their appearance; it's what's in the heart that matters. Hope you enjoy the short story.

On a hot sunny day in July while walking in the park; Janice sat under a large oak tree and meditated on her life. The sun was shining bright and the birds were humming sweetly. Janice grew up in a very hostile environment most of her life. Reflecting back on her life, she realized that she was brought up poorly. At the age of 4 years old, she was told that the only man that has taken care of her was killed by a drunk driver. She really could not comprehend that at that time but, when she was older; it was devastating to her. The only people that she knew were her immediate family. Being in the park gave her a real peace of mind. While sitting there daydreaming, a young man passed by; not so dressed up, beard, long sleeves shirt and baggy jeans. Janice eyes gazed as he walked by. She reflected back on her past as he walked by. The outer appearance of his garments reminded her of her childhood. As he passed, there was a nice aroma of cologne flowing through the air; it's an aroma that she will not forget anytime soon. She almost could not take her eyes off of him. Well she stayed in the park for a few more hours and then decided to start home; the sun was about to go down.

Janice was a person that loves to perfect everything. Her family would always tell her she was very anal. Janice was an executive secretary for this large firm in New York. This city was very different from where she lived previously. She came from a smaller town where everyone knew each other. This environment was very new to her. Well, Janice always goes to lunch at this place called: The Hungry Feast Buffet. This particular day, she decided not to be so anal, so she sat at a table by the window where she could see all the traffic going by. As the waiter came to take her order, she smelled the same aroma that she did in the park as this gentlemen passed by. He passed so swiftly that she did not get a chance to see his face. She immediately asked the waitress, "Who is that gentlemen? The waitress stated, "I don't know, but he is one of our regulars." Janice became very curious about this gentleman because of the aroma. The gentleman sat about 5 tables across the room. As Janice head weaved and bobbed, trying to get a better look at the gentlemen's face, he suddenly turned around and they looked at each other face to face for about 3 seconds. Janice heart began racing and she became very nervous. After she ate her lunch, she stood up to leave; she could feel as if someone was staring at her. She slightly glanced back, and it was the gentlemen looking at her as she left the building. She got a better look at his face; he still had a beard, long sleeves, slacks, but his eyes were outstanding; they were these warm brown eyes of a teddy bear. It was something about this gentleman that she could not put her hand on.

The next day at work, as Janice proceeded to push the button for the elevator, she and a gentleman's hand touched the elevator button at the same time. Janice said, "Excuse me", without looking up, but she smelled the aroma of his cologne. As she looked up, it was the same gentlemen from the restaurant looking at her with those teddy bear eyes, and he gently said; "Hello, how are you doing? Janice answered nervously, "Fine." He said, "My name is Teddy. Janice asked, are you the gentleman I saw in the restaurant on yesterday, he said, "Yes I'm." Janice then said, "Were you in the park on yesterday also? He said, "Yes, how did you know that was me?" She said, "The scent of your cologne was so breath taking." He said," I'm glad you liked it." They continued talking, and then he asked what floor was she going to, she said, the 21st, he said, "So am I." They began discussing their jobs and what they did. They found out that they had a lot in common. Well as they got off the elevator and went their separate ways, Janice realized that she did not give Teddy her name. Janice decided that she would give Teddy her name the next time she sees him since she knows they work on the same floor."

While sitting at home doing paperwork from the job, Janice decided to call her friend Stacey, who also works in the same office complex. Janice and Stacey both went to College at New York State. After a few years, they went their separate ways, but just a few months ago, they bumped into each other in the office complex where they both are now employed. Stacey was Janice's childhood friend. Even though Janice and Stacey worked in the same office building, they did not see very much of each other, but spoke occasionally in person and on the phone. Janice and Stacey's lives had change dramatically. Over the past few years, Janice went back to college to get her masters degree in Business Administration. Stacey went to school, but did not finish due to situations arising in her life, but eventually she received her degree. Stacey had a lot that has happened to her over the years. Stacey has become a very critical and negative person because of situations in life. Stacey hung out with older women who introduced her to the streets. Stacey use to be a Call-Girl working on the New York Strip making lots of money until one day a gentlemen that she met was not so nice to her. She was raped and beaten; it has really given her a bad complex with men for a long time, but she is trying to work through that. Stacey has never mentioned this to Janice. As Janice began to tell

Stacey about this gentleman at work, Stacey interrupted her and asked, "Do you like this guy? Janice stated, "I do and I know that I'm attracted to him; I can tell the moment we looked into each other's eyes." Stacey as if she already knew Teddy and they only talked a short while and realized that they had a lot in common. Stacey wanted to know when Janice would see Teddy again. Janice told Stacey she wasn't sure, and they really met by accident. Janice asked Stacey if she was in a relationship, Stacey just said, "Not at this time". Janice did not find that to be strange because Stacey did not date often during their school years. Well, it was getting late so Janice told Stacey that she would keep her updated on the situation between her and Teddy. As Janice laid there in her bed looking at the ceiling, she could not get Teddy off her mind. She thought about calling him, only if she had a last name; well it was a nice thought.

As Janice woke up the next day, she decided to do something different with her hair. She realized that if she was attracted to this guy, she wanted to look very nice whenever she seen him again. She was going to get out of the normal routine that she does daily. When she arrived at work, she saw Teddy standing at the elevator as if he was waiting for her. She began getting that nervous feeling again; she knew without a doubt that she was attracted to him. He said, "Good morning". She said, "Good Morning, how are you? He said, "Alright, now that I have seen you." She was blushing on the inside. He told her how nice her hair looked. He then said," I forget to get your name last time we spoke." She said, "Janice Right." They continued talking as they entered the elevator and he finally asked the question, "Are you dating anyone"? Janice quickly said, "No, not at the moment." Teddy told her that he did not want to make any fast advances towards her, but he thought she was vey attractive. He told her that he had two tickets to a concert that he had won, and wanted to know if she would like to go on a date. She almost could not wait until he completed the question, she said, "Yes." You could see the sparkle in Janice's eyes and Teddy's chest sticking out. They exchanged information and Teddy said he would pick her up around 7 p.m. that evening. They departed and went to their departments. Janice felt like screaming with joy; she could hardly get work done thinking about the date later that evening with Teddy.

When she arrived home after work, she began cleaning up her house because she knew Teddy was coming to pick her up later. She put on soft music to set the mood while getting ready. As she began getting dressed for the big night, she sat alongside the bed and put on her most elegant smelling perfume. She put on her dazzling diamond earrings, with this fitted A-line black dress and black stilettos. Suddenly the doorbell rang; she walked slowly to the door and thought, "It could be no one else but Teddy." When she opened the door, there stood Teddy with a nice black tailored suit, gold cuff links, and a dark brown shirt to match those teddy bear brown eyes. He looked much different from when she saw him in the park and at the restaurant. As he walked in, he said, "You look very stunning;" she said," So do you." He gave her a soft hug, like a real gentleman. After a few minutes, they were ready to go. As they left out of the house, outside was a Champagne BMW 321 Series with black leather interior. Janice was shocked considering the way she seen him previously. She was very impressed. She would not have thought he would have something so luxurious, but he did.

As they approached the car, Teddy said, "Let me get that for you." He was such a gentleman, I felt like a queen. About 10 minutes into the drive, he asked me was I comfortable because he wanted things just right for me. As we were riding to our destination, which was about 20 - 30 minutes away; he had soft music playing; which set the atmosphere for romance. Teddy began asking Janice to tell him a little about herself and she told him that she was more of a casual person, likes having fun and someday wants to get married and settle down. She also told him of some of the things that she like to do. Then she said, 'Tell me something about you." He began by saying that; he is originally from Los Angeles, California, but his business has moved him to New York. He said that he was the only child and the CEO of one of the largest film producing companies in this part of the United States. He immediately said, "I don't say that to be bragging; I just feel comfortable enough to tell you that." He said, "Many people don't know that about me because I know who he I am and I don't believe I have to prove myself to anyone." Janice felt so bad at that point, because she pre-judged him based on the way he was dressed when she first seen him in the park and second at the restaurant.

Finally they arrived at the concert; he said, "Don't move I will open the door for you." Janice felt so alive because all the other guys that she has dated never done anything like this. As they walked into the concert, people were looking at them as if they were the perfect couple. As they approached their seats, he pulled her chair out for her. Performing in concert was and old band which turned out to be their favorite. To say they have not been knowing each other that long they have a lot in common. Janice was very excited because she had not been to a concert in quite some time. As the evening went on; the band performed a slow jam which set the mood. Teddy said, "I know we haven't known each other that long, but I feel as if we've known each other forever." "I know this is very unusual for me, but I have never felt this way before for anyone so soon." Teddy asked Janice, "Do you believe in love at first sight? Janice said, "Yes, I do because you will know in your heart because it feels right." Teddy stood up in front of Janice, he then bent down on one knee. Janice hand went over her mouth because she could not believe what she was seeing. Teddy then said," Will You Marry Me?" She could do nothing but stare into his brown eyes, and her lips parted and said, "Yes". Then he took her face and gently turned it towards him and gave her a soft kiss as he looked into her eyes with those teddy bear eyes. That kissed made Janice close her eyes and want to stay in that moment forever. As Janice begins to cry, Teddy said, "I hope those are tears of joy;" Janice said, 'they are." After the concert was over, Teddy and Janice drove to his place to have a celebration drink. This was Janice first time going to Teddy's home. As they drove up; they drove up this drive-way shaped like a horseshoe. Janice eyes gazed at the beauty of it all. His house sat upon a hill and it was very huge. As they walked in, there was a mirror that reflects them as they walked through the door. As the mirror reflected them, Teddy said, "This is the way I seen us, together." He already had the champagne on ice with two glasses and a rose. Janice was amazed as she looked around his home. She was marveled at how beautiful it was. They sat down on the sofa beside each other and Teddy began to tell her; "I knew you were the one because I prayed about this." I asked God to give me peace in my spirit when Ms. Right comes along. He said, "I have been attracted to other women, but not at first sight; it was something different about you. She found out not only was he a gentleman, but a Christian man that believes in prayer. She then told Teddy that she had a confession to make; he said, "I know, you pre-judged me according to my outer appearance. She couldn't say anything but," forgive me." He said, "That is why I dress the way I do because I want a person to accept me for who I'm and not for what I have."

The night was getting late and Teddy had to take Janice home. As Teddy drove Janice home, they just were expressing to each other how happy they were to have found each other. When they arrived at Janice's home, Teddy opened the door for Janice and walked her to the door, gave her a soft kiss and he left. After Janice made it home, she immediately called her friend Stacey and told her the good news, so she thought. Stacey seemed very reluctant in saying, "Are you sure you are not moving too fast?" Janice hesitated because she would never have thought Stacey would say anything like that; she ignored it and said, "No, I know he is the one for me." Stacey then said, "O.K., if you're happy, I'm happy." Janice did not like her tone but did not say anything. Janice then asked Stacey if she would be her Maid of Honor, Stacey said, "Yes." Janice thought in the back of her mind, "surely Stacey would not be a little jealous." Since Teddy and Janice knew that they wanted to get married, all was left to do is to set a time and a date. They were set to be married in a few weeks. Meanwhile, Janice and her best friend Stacey were going to begin shopping for a wedding dress. Janice was not a very high maintenance person, but she wanted to look real nice on her wedding day. Janice wanted an elegant but simple wedding. Even though Teddy was wealthy, she was not going to be too extravagant. Sometimes weddings can be much of wasteful spending; just for show. Everyone at work was excited for Janice. Stacey decided that she and her co-workers would give Janice a surprise bridal shower at her home. Stacey and the other co-workers met on several occasions to plan the shower. Well, the evening of the shower, Stacey picked Janice up at home after work and they decided to go to the bridal store while their co-workers decorated for the shower at Stacey's home. While at the bridal store, Janice eyes caught a nice dress with a V-shaped train with beads and lace at the top. Janice said, "This is the perfect dress." Stacey told Janice to try the dress on and when Janice stepped out; Stacey said, "Perfect." Janice decided to get the dress instead of looking other places. Janice and Teddy also decided to get married at his home since it was very large and that is where they will reside. As they arrived at Stacey's place; Janice saw many vehicles and asked Stacey," What was going on with all these cars?" "Stacey said "I have no idea; I guess everyone decided to visit this area today." As they entered into Stacey's apartment, it was rather dark. Stacey told Janice to stand at the door until she put the lights on. When Stacey put the lights on, everyone yelled, "Surprise." You should have seen the look on Janice's face. She was so surprised at what they had done, and the biggest part is she did not have a clue what was going on. Well, they showed great hospitality to Janice. They catered food and it was very good. Her friends did not allow her to do anything but sit down and be waited on because this was a very special occasion. Janice eyes were filled with tears as she began to give a speech about the shower. She said, "I'm so thankful to have friends like you, I don't take your kindness lightly; I appreciate everything you have done for me." Then everyone came in and gave a group hug. Stacey said, "Let's put on some music and dance." Janice said that she liked old music, so Stacey put on this song that Janice liked. They laughed and talked about old times; Janice was having one of the best times of her life. Well, it was getting late and everyone wanted to get home before the traffic gets too bad. Everyone said their good-byes and went their separate ways. That left Stacey and Janice there alone. As Janice walked around Stacey's apartment, she noticed Stacey in a picture that was very shocking to Janice. Before Janice could as any questions, Stacey immediately took the picture and put it away. She kiddingly said, "That picture was from my younger days." Janice was puzzled by that picture, but never said anything else to Stacey about it. As Stacey was in route to take Janice home, Janice's phone rang; it was Teddy. Stacey could hear the echo of Teddy talking off the phone. He asked Janice, how was her day; Janice replied, "It was great". Janice was snickering and laughing as Teddy told her sweet things, but out the corner of her eye she could see Stacey rolling her eyes as if she was getting sick of hearing Janice laugh. Janice could not believe it, but she notice it only happens when she talks about Teddy or talking to Teddy around Stacey. Janice told Teddy that she will call him when she gets home.

As they pulled up in front of Janice's home, Stacey helped Janice take her gifts from the bridal shower into her home. Janice invited Stacey to stay and have a cup of coffee; Janice wanted to talk about the picture that she seen earlier at Stacey's house. Stacey was very reluctant; and said, "I have to get home because it's getting late." Janice was a little stunned because that wasn't the first time Stacey's tone of voice was like that. After Janice got relaxed and ready for bed, she called Teddy and told him how Stacey was acting towards her. Teddy said, "Sometimes when people say they are happy for you, they are really not." Janice wanted to know how to deal with someone that has been her best friend for so many years and all of a sudden it seems as though Stacey is Jealous of her when this is one of the happiest times in her life. Well a few weeks have already gone by and it's a few more weeks left before the big day. Janice hasn't heard from Stacey so she decided to call her but no one answered; that has happened several times. Janice was noticing that Stacey was not answering her calls, but when she did talk with her, her excuse was that she was busy. Janice decided to ride to Stacey's home, but right before you get to her street, you can see her home. Stacey was sating outside with two other ladies. Janice decided to call to see if Stacey would answer the phone; the phone rang several times and all of a sudden Stacey looked at her phone and showed her friends as she hung up the phone. Janice eyes filled with tears as she drove off. Later that night Janice could not fall asleep so she began to pray about the situation between her and Stacey; this was very disturbing for her. She did not need all this with her big wedding day coming up. Janice decided to start distancing herself from Stacey until they can sort out this misunderstanding of feelings.

The following day at work Janice was approached by her co-workers that were at the bridal shower. They let her know how they enjoyed themselves. As she looked around, there was Stacey sitting at her desk. One of the co-workers asked Stacey was she o.k.; Stacey said, "Yes." Janice being the person she is decided that she was going to approach Stacey about this situation. After work Janice saw Stacey walking to her car. Janice said, "Hey Stacey, wait up." Janice asked her how has she been doing; Stacey told her she's been fine, just has a lot going on. Janice said, "I have been calling you but the phone just rang." Janice really wanted to see if Stacey would tell her the truth, so she said,

"I drove by your house, but you had company outside." Stacey had a strange look on her face like, she wondered if Janice seen her purposely not answering her phone. Stacey said; "I have to be honest with you; I'm a little jealous of the relationship you and Teddy have; it's not that I want Teddy, but it's like once you get married I'm going to lose my best friend." Janice assured Stacy that they will always be friends no matter what. Janice hugged Stacey as she began to cry. Stacey said, "I wish I was as happy as you are." Janice told Stacey that you have to be happy within yourself and not to look for people to determine your happiness. Janice said, "I'm glad we had this talk because my wedding is a few weeks away." Stacey seemed so relieved that she told Janice what she was feeling. Janice told Stacey they will began looking for the colors for her wedding. Stacey said, "Do you know what colors you want for your wedding?" Janice said Tan, Brown, and Pink."

The next day Janice and Stacey met after work at Michaels to pick out the flower arrangements. Stacey did not know Janice was bringing Teddy along to meet her. Teddy wanted to meet this person that Janice spoke so highly of. Janice introduced Teddy to Stacey; Teddy said, "I'm glad Janice has a friend that she is close to." Stacey commented and said, "I'm glad for you and Janice, she deserves someone that loves her." Teddy decided to take Janice and Stacey out to dinner before they went shopping. After dinner, Teddy decided that he would go and let the ladies hang out. Stacey told Teddy that she will bring Janice home after they were finish shopping. As Teddy got ready to leave, he reached over and shook Stacey's hand and said, "It was a pleasure to meet you." Janice stood up as Teddy got up to leave. Teddy softly grabbed Janice around her waist and pulled her to him and kissed her softly on her lips. Stacey looked as she grabbed her chest and said, "Oh, he is so sweet to you." Janice and Stacey left the restaurant in route to Michael's. Stacey made a wrong turn and went a few blocks out of the way in the other direction. While in route, back towards Michael, there was a vehicle just like Teddy's; same color and all. Stacey, immediately said, "Is that Teddy?" Janice with a soft voice said," No Teddy is on his way home." Stacey then said, "Are you sure?" Janice said, "I trust Teddy?" Stacey was really trying to convince Janice that was Teddy, so she drove pass Michael's to get to the red light to discover that was not Teddy. Stacey looked as if she was sad about it. Janice never said anything, but noticed the expression on Stacey's face. Janice thought to herself, "I wonder if Stacey thinks Teddy would cheat on me. Well, they finally arrived at Michael's. As they began to shop for flowers, Stacey asked Janice, "Does Teddy have any friends?" Janice told Stacey that she has met a few of his friends once or twice. Janice look puzzled as she thought," I wonder if Stacey is looking to get married." She asked Stacey, "Do you want to get married one day." Stacey immediately said, "Oh no, the life I'm living is good enough for me." As Janice looked at Stacey's facial expressions they were saying something else, but Janice did not say anything. Janice and Stacey stayed in the store for a few hours until they found the perfect flowers. As Janice and Stacey approached the counter, Janice said, "I have misplaced the credit card that Teddy's given me to pay for the wedding items." Stacey said surprisingly, "He gives you his credit cards?" Janice said, "Teddy is a true gentleman." Janice was getting vibes that Stacey did not like that very much. As Stacey and Janice left the store and on their way to take Janice home, Janice decided to go to Teddy's house instead of going home. Janice never told Stacey that Teddy was wealthy because she did not want her judging him or judging her. As they drove up to Teddy's house, Stacey's mouth dropped as we drove around the horseshoe driveway. Stacey said, "Is Teddy rich?" Janice said, "He's just a hard worker." Janice was very skeptical about letting Stacey know where Teddy lives because she doesn't want her to become even more jealous.

Janice had to invite Stacey inside to show her where the wedding was going to take place and what needed to be decorated. Stacey was amazed at the elegance of the house. After she showed Stacey everything, she then walked her to her car and Stacey went on her way.

As Stacey and Janice spoke in between days; Stacey continued commenting on Teddy's house and wish one day she could have something like that. Days went by and the wedding was closing in. Stacey decided to take the day off work before the wedding so she could decorate. Stacey did not let Janice know she was going over to Teddy's house; after all she wanted it to be a surprise. As Stacey drove up to the house, she saw Teddy's vehicle in the driveway. Stacey was not dressed very appropriately while going to her best friend's fiancé's house. Stacey rang the doorbell and Teddy opened the door. He was surprised to see Stacey and immediately asked her, "What are you doing here? She said, "I'm here to decorate for the wedding." He immediately said," Does Janice know your here?" Stacey said, I want to surprise her and have everything decorated early. Teddy didn't seem too pleased with what Stacey said, but he went on. Teddy showed Stacey the place that was to be decorated. Stacey asked Teddy if he wouldn't mind if she asked him a question. Stacey asked Teddy, "What type of man are you really?" Teddy replied, "What do you mean?" She said, "I know you love Janice, but would you cheat on her?" Teddy said, "What type of question is that, and why are you asking?" Stacey said, "I'm just looking out for my friend. Teddy said, "Or are you looking out for her or for yourself?" Teddy said, "I love Janice and I look out for her, so I done a back ground check on you." Teddy told Stacey that he found out that she had been arrested for prostitution. You should have seen the shock on Stacey's face because Teddy knew something about her past that she has been trying to keep hidden, especially from Janice. Teddy was a little upset by that time, so he asked Stacey to leave. He felt Stacey was judging him by the things he had. Stacey said, "It's best if Janice doesn't know we had this conversation." Teddy said, "I think it's best if you don't attend our wedding; and I will make sure Janice understands why you will not be there." Later that evening Janice called Stacey to see if there were anything else needed for the wedding. Stacey told Janice that she had things that she has not told her regarding the picture at her home, but she will find out soon enough. Stacy said, "I won't be able to make the wedding; an emergency came up and I have to leave town." Janice said, "But you are my Maid of Honor." Stacey apologized to Janice and hung up the phone. Janice was frantic so she immediately called Teddy. Teddy said, "I was going to call you and talk to you about your friend Stacey." Janice said, "Do you know something I don't know?" Teddy explained the situation to Janice and told her Stacey loves her but she is jealous of her. He also told her that Stacey was a Call Girl on the New York Strip. Janice said, "That explains the picture at Stacey's house." Janice could not believe this. Janice began crying while talking to Teddy, he reassured Janice that everything was going to be alright and they will get through this together. Janice said, "I can't call the wedding off and I don't have a maid of honor." Teddy told Janice that he would take care of it. The very next day, when Janice went to lunch, Teddy went to her department to speak with her co-work Susie. Susie was at Janice's bridal shower. Teddy asked Susie if she would be Janice's Maid of Honor. He did not go into detail as to why Stacey could not do it. Susie was so surprised, she began to cry, because no one has ever asked her to be a Maid of Honor. Teddy was happy that Susie agreed to do it. Teddy asked Susie to keep this their secret because he wanted Janice to be surprised. Later that evening, Janice called Teddy and thanked him for being there for her. She was very shocked at Stacey's past. She was not judging her, but never thought that Stacey would go that way.

Anyway, Janice decided she was not going to let anything mess up her big day, which is on tomorrow.

As Janice awoke with the sounds of the birds and the sun shining through the bay windows; she sat up alongside the bed. She reflected back a few months ago when she was alone. She then, kneeled down on her knees to thank God for all of her blessings that he had given her. Janice's mind wandered as she thought about the wedding. She began to wonder how the entire wedding was going to turn out since her best friend left town at the last minute. She then took a deep breath and said, "I will trust God, he has given me an honest finance; he will take care of me. Janice decided that she wasn't going to do too much today, just relax. As the day went on, the time began dwindling and getting closer to the start of the wedding. Janice began laying out her dress and other things that will go with the wedding dress, Janice has no one to help her get dress, so she thought. There was a knock at the door; it was her co-worker Susie. She told Janice that Teddy came by and spoke with her and asked if she would be a backup just in case something went wrong. All Janice could do was hug Susie. While Susie began to help Janice get dressed, she said, "We need something old, something new, something borrowed, and something blue." After getting all those things, Janice was dressed and ready to walk down the aisle. Before leaving the room, Susie told Janice to look in the mirror and see how beautiful she was. Janice was very pleased with her appearance. As she entered the wedding area, there were a lot of people there; Janice was very surprised. Teddy requested Janice favorite band from the concert there in person to perform their favorite song. The moment the band began singing, brought back memories of the first time that they met. As Janice walked down the aisle with tears of love streaming down her face; as she faced Teddy, with tears in his eyes; he softly said, "I know a man is not supposed to cry, but you are worth crying for." The minister himself took a deep breath, because it was so touching. After the wedding, there was a large reception next to the pool. The reception went on for a few hours, but Teddy and Janice decided that they would not go on a honeymoon since they had everything they needed at home. After all the guest left, the phone rang; it was Stacey. She wanted to wish Janice and Teddy many happy years on their marriage. Janice being the person she is, told Stacey that she is sorry for everything that has taken place and that maybe one day they can make amends. Stacey decided that she will move away and start over again. Janice told Stacey that everyone makes mistakes and people deserve a second chance. Stacey was glad to hear Janice say that. They talked a few more minutes and then hung up the phone. Teddy and Janice will now began their new life. They both came to an agreement and decided not to have children but to deposit the love that they had for each other into the lives of others.

9 Robbing and Stealing Of the Heart and Mind

Clarence was a married man that has a reputation for dating other women. He finds this one lady friend that he really falls for. Delilah and Mary are good friends. Mary was a classmate of Clarence. Clarence was always up to no-good, but he will learn a great lesson on how to treat women. One thing you don't do is play with a person's heart or mind.

Clarence was a city slicker and Delilah was a country cougar. These two mixed will cause a mudslide. There is a difference between robbing and stealing. When someone robs you; you see them, but when someone one steals from you; you don't see them. Quit taking advice from someone who is defeated (the devil). If someone breaks into your home to rob you, you would do everything in your power to protect yourself. Well God had given us this earthen vessel (our body) and the Devil knocks on the door (through our thoughts.) Once we open that door he begin to work on stealing everything God has put in us to be victorious in this life. He began to rob us of our joy, peace, and relationships. We need to load the word of God and call on the name of Jesus. Clarence robbed Delilah of her joy, peace and relationships. He stole her heart and she will almost loose her mind when she finds out the double life he was leading. He was in her presence robbing her because he was able to get into her head, but she did not see it coming when he stole her heart, but he did not see it either when she stole his mind. See People will sometimes cause you to become something that you are not for a season. He had her, but she had him also. It's a danger when you play heart and mind games. So what was the reason for the relationship in the first place; well keep reading and you will find out;

it's not what you see on the outside, but it is what on the inside.

Delilah was a young lady from a small town way up north called chosen few. See this town consisted on no more than 400 people so that meant everyone was familiar with one another. Delilah was single, had never been married and was a very God-fearing woman. She spent her time working, going to church and just enjoying herself on the weekends with friends and family. This one particular day, she went to the library to do some research. As she sat quietly in the back of the library, she noticed a young gentlemen looking at the books as if he was trying to find a particular book. The gentlemen did not look familiar to her so she said, "Excuse me sir, may I be of assistance to you." He said, "I'm looking for a particular book called "All or Nothing". Delilah said, "That sounds like an interesting book." The gentlemen said, "One of my friends told me about it and I wanted to read it for myself." She said, "You're not from around here are you?" He said, "No, is it that obvious." She said, "Well, this town being so small, we can recognize a visitor a mile away." He said, "I'm sorry, my name is Clarence; I'm just passing through on my way to my cousin house about 1 hour up the road." She said, "My name is Delilah." Once Clarence got the book, he asked Delilah if it was alright to sit at the table with her. They sat peacefully and talked briefly. Well, it was getting late and Delilah had to get home and Clarence had to get on the road. Clarence told Delilah how nice it was to meet her; Delilah told him the same about him. As they departed, Clarence said, "Do you mind if I stop back by on my way back from my cousin?" Delilah said, "Well, I don't think that is a good ideal being I just met you, but it was nice meeting you." Clarence had a surprised look on his face because he never gets turned down by most women. This may be a challenge for him. Well a few days went by and Clarence and his cousin were outside talking. He asked his cousin do he ever go to chosen few. His cousin said, "No, they have all those religious women up there and they don't talk to anybody." Clarence told his cousin how he met this young lady and she was very kind. Clarence is trying to figure out a way to go back to see Delilah. Clarence told his cousin since he was going to be there for a few weeks, they may ride to chosen few over the weekend; his cousin agreed. Well when the time came for Clarence and his cousin to go to chosen few, his cousin decided that he was going to drive. As they were driving they began talking about the book called, "All or Nothing." Clarence wanted his cousin to give him a view of the book and what is was about. His cousin said that the title speaks for itself. He said, "The person in this story got everything that he wanted." There was a smirk that came on Clarence's face. He said, "I must read this book before I go back in a few weeks." Well they arrived in Chosen Few and there was a carnival at the fair grounds. Clarence and his cousin walked around. All the while, Clarence was hoping he would see Delilah. He wanted to ask some of the other people, but he was uneasy in doing so. They stayed there half the day, but he never got a chance to see Delilah. On the way back to his cousin's house, Clarence got a little anxious about reading the book, so when they arrived back at his cousin's house, Clarence stayed up late reading. He read the entire book and was really impressed. He could see himself being the person in the book. Well the weekend has come to an end and Clarence had to get back home to take care of some business. He thought in his mind that he could not go back home without seeing Delilah again. He remembered the time in which they were at the library and he had to bring he book back also. He took his chance and went to the library. While checking the book back in, he looked up and Delilah was coming through the door. As she looked up and saw him she was just as surprised as he was. This was such an odd moment since Delilah only met Clarence one time. Anyway, Clarence started up a conversation and they sat down at the table and talked. Clarence was trying to get to know Delilah a little better, but Delilah was very distant and said very little. Delilah made up in her mind a long time ago that she wanted a God-Fearing man and she was not settling. She did not know much about Clarence, but she was going to find out. Being in such a small town, the crime was very low. As Delilah stood up to leave, Clarence asked could he walk her to her car; she agreed. When they arrived at the car, Delilah unlocked her door. Clarence said," Let me get the door for you, "I can at least be a gentleman since you won't give me your telephone number." She said, "I don't give out my number to everyone, but I will give you my last name." She wanted to see how interested Clarence was in her and how far he would go to get her telephone number without her giving it to him. That would show Delilah how interested he is in her. A few weeks passed by and she had not heard from Clarence. She began thinking about him and in her heart she wanted him to find her telephone number because she wanted him to call her. She found herself going back to the library reminiscing about the last time they saw each other. She knew he was gone back to his home, but she was just hoping she would see him. She knew a connection had taken place when she saw him the second time. She stayed at the library until her normal time and she went home. She began watching a movie on television and began dozing off when the telephone rang. She was half asleep when she picked the phone up. Clarence said, "Hello is this Delilah?" Delilah's eyes lit up and she said, "Clarence is this you?" He said, "yes it is; it was tough, but I got your telephone number." She was smiling from ear to ear. They talked for a while before hanging up. The very next day, Delilah got up and done her normal routine, but as she prayed this time, she prayed for a relationship with Clarence. As time went on Clarence began coming to Chosen few to see Delilah on a regular basis at the library. Delilah was afraid to let him come to her home just yet. Delilah decided that if she was going to let Clarence come to her home and be in her life she will need to do a back ground check on him. She had one of her friends at the police department to run a report. It would take a few days to learn the results. Delilah was very anxious to know if there were any secrets about Clarence that she needed to know. The background check came back and there wasn't anything nothing on the report to alarm Delilah. She had a sigh of relief. Clarence was coming down that weekend and Delilah was going to invite him to her home for the first time. When Clarence arrived at the library, Delilah stayed in her car. Clarence came to the window and as he reached to open her door; she said, "Get in,

I'm taking you to my home for dinner." Clarence had this big smile come on his face while getting in the car. In route to her home, Clarence asked Delilah, "May I ask what made you take me to your home for dinner?" She said, "After I ran a background check and it came back good, I said, " I believe that you are a good person. " Clarence said, "No one has ever done a background check on me before." Delilah said, "You can't just trust anybody." As they arrived at Delilah's home; Clarence got out and opened the door for her. As they walked into the house, the aroma of the food was in the air. Clarence said, "The food really smells delicious, what is it?" Delilah said, "I want it to be a surprise." Clarence was very helpful in helping Delilah set the table for their meal. Delilah and Clarence ate dinner and wash dishes afterwards. Clarence said, "How about we watch a movie since it's still early; Delilah agreed. As they were watching the movie, Clarence slowly put his arm around Delilah's neck, but that made Delilah uncomfortable. It had been a long time since Delilah dated anyone. She nervously said, "How about I take you back to your car." He said, "I'm sorry if I offended you." She said, I'm just a little nervous right now and we may be moving too fast." While in route to his vehicle, Deliah was very quiet. Clarence said, "I'm sorry, it wont' happen again; we can take this as slow as you want to."

Delilah said, "Thanks". Once they arrived at his car she told him good night and drove off. Clarence was a little upset because he is a type of man that is use to getting his way. He can not let her see that side of him; it was too early in the relationship. Delilah thought about what she told Clarence and she thought in her mind that she may have reacted too fast; after all it was only a hug. She is really trying to guard her heart so she will not get hurt like the past relationships. Clarence has begun going to chosen few every weekend. As time went on, Delilah began to loosen up a little and began doing little things like holding hands with Clarence. Delilah decided that the next time Clarence comes down that they would go out of town. The weekend had finally come and Delilah was anxious to see Clarence because she was going to let him know she wanted to go out of town. Delilah asked Clarence if it was alright if they went to his hometown. Clarence kind of hesitated, but he agreed. He did not want to disagree and make Delilah upset or suspicious of him. When they arrived in town, Delilah asked Clarence to take her to the Drug Store to get some sinus medicine. Clarence waited in the car while Delilah went into the drug store. There were things that Clarence has not shared with Delilah like he was married , he did not think is should be mentioned at the time. Clarence was well-known in his hometown. His father- in- law worked as the pharmacist in the Drug Store in which Delilah went in. While in the store, there were two ladies in there talking about the latest gossip. It was about this couple having a messy marriage. Delilah being the person she was did not like gossip, so she checked out and left the store. When she returned to the car; Clarence was sitting there with this baseball cap on his head. Delilah thought it was cute. As they drove down the street; a man yelled out and said, "Hey how's the wife?" Delilah said, "Did he say, how is your wife?" Clarence said, "No, "he said how is your life." That was a close call for Clarence. The gentlemen that yelled at Clarence did not know the he and his wife was going through a divorce; neither did Delilah. They stayed in his hometown for a few hours, but before getting on the road, they decided to stop at a burger house; one of those places that sold old fashion burgers. While they were there many people that knew Clarence came by and spoke. As they were eating, Delilah said, "Clarence, tell me a little about you." Clarence said, "What is it you want to know?" Delilah asked Clarence if he had been married before. Clarence said, "Yes, but that was a long time ago." Delilah found it kind of awkward that he answered so quickly like it agitated him. She did not think much about it since she done a back ground check on him; what could be so bad if he had anything to hide, she was thinking. As they headed back to Chosen Few; Delilah told Clarence that she was sorry for overreacting the other day. With a smirk on his face, Clarence said," I understand you were just taking it slow." As they drove further up the road , Clarence suggested they stop and take a break since it was still early in the day. Being the gentlemen he was, he opened the door for Delilah and took her by the hand. As she got out of the car, he gently embraced her against his chest. Delilah became a little flushed said, "Wow, you are such a gentlemen." As they walked down the trail, the sun was shining, the breeze was blowing and the birds were singing. They came upon this huge oak tree with lots of shade; they sat down and just looked at nature. Clarence decided that this was his opportunity to kiss Delilah. To keep her trust, he asked, "May I kiss you?" She said, "Yes, I thought you would never ask." "Delilah felt she was enjoying the kiss too much so she pushed him away. He said, "Just relax, she said, "I think it is time we go." Delilah has never met anyone this kind and respectful to her. While driving down the highway, Clarence could see Delilah looking at him, so he turned to look at her, but she quickly turned her head. He knew then that she was falling for him. They finally arrived in Chosen Few; as they pulled up to Delilah's home, Clarence walked her to the door. Delilah said, “Would you like to come in?” Clarence said, “I want us to take it slow.” That really impressed Delilah because most men would have not passed up the opportunity. Delilah did not know that Clarence was very manipulating. Everything she needed to know about Clarence was not in the police report. Delilah felt the relationship has gone to another level. In the coming week Deliah decides that she will surprise Clarence and go to his home town. She decided that if she was going to be dating Clarence she needed to get familiar with his home town. When she arrived in town, she was a little lost because she only been there once. Delilah decided to stop by this Café and call Clarence to come and meet her. When she called Clarence, he took a while to answer the phone. When Clarence finally answered the phone, it was a little noisy in the back ground, Delilah said; "Hey are you busy, he said, "I'm never too busy for you." Delilah said, "I have a surprise for you, before he could answer, she said, "I'm in town." He kind of stumbled over his words and said, "What are you doing here?" She said, "I wanted to surprise you." She said I'm at this Cafe on 3rd street; I wanted to take you out to lunch." Clarence made an excuse that he was tied up and she should have called before dropping in. That caught Delilah’s off guard because she did not expect that from Clarence. Being such a small town, everybody was acquainted with each other. Delilah was a little disappointed; so when the waitress passed back, she decided to order some food. The waitress saw the disappointment on her face and asked, "Are you o.k.?" Delilah said, "I'm fine, came to surprise my male friend, but he is tied up at the moment. The waitress said, "I'm about to go on break, do you mind some company?" Delilah said, "That would be great." As they sat at the table, Delilah said, "So what's your name", "she said, Mary." Mary asked, so have you and your male friend been seeing each other for a while?" Delilah said, "For a few months." Mary said, "This is a small town, I may know him, what is his name?" Delilah said, "Clarence". Mary snickered, "You mean Clarence the stud." Delilah said, "What is that supposed to mean?" Mary said, "Well you know how men are with women." She said, "No tell me. She said, "Everyone knows that Clarence is married and going through a divorce." Delilah's eyes got very big. Mary said, "By the look on your face, I guess you did not know that." Delilah said, " I have to go." Mary said, "I'm sorry, but I thought you knew. While in route back home, Delilah decided to call Clarence. He did not answer the phone so she left him a message. She told him she never want to see him again and to have a good life. Tears began to roll down her face and she began crying hysterically; until she had to pull off the road to safety. So many thoughts were going through Delilah's mind. She realized that she was being played by Clarence the stud. Delilah thought to herself; I knew this was too good to be true. She was angry and wanted Clarence to pay for the way she is feeling right now, but she knew that was not the right thing to do. She realized that Clarence robbed her mind and stole her heart. After Clarence received her message he tried calling her several times, but Delilah refused to answer the phone. In her mind, she was wondering why Clarence didn't tell her he was married. As time went on she and Clarence has not spoken in a few weeks. She was really missing him and was hoping he called because she wanted to speak with him, but refused to call him. Men know that when women are upset, they have to give them plenty of time to cool off. By this time another week has gone by. Tonight was an early night for Delilah to get off work so she decided to pick up dinner and rent a movie. As she sat watching the movie, the telephone rings, it was Clarence. She let the phone ring at least 3 times before she picked it up. Clarence was concerned about the reason she was upset, but she did not want to talk about it over the phone. Clarence made a decision that he would come over one weekend and they would talk about it. When a person has a past that is not much different from yours they tend to not hold a grudge. Delilah may be from a small town, but because Clarence does not know anyone else besides her, it's easy to get away with your past. As time went on, Delilah made several trips to Clarence's home town, without him knowing. Delilah and Mary were becoming good friends. Mary kept Delilah informed on what Clarence has been doing. Mary did not know that Delilah was just trying to pay Clarence back for not telling her that he was married. Delilah felt as if Clarence made a fool out of her. Delilah had to see things for herself before she confront him with anything and did not want Mary involved. It was on a Friday night during the hot summer when Delilah received a phone call from Mary. Mary told Delilah they were having their annual fair and thought this was a good time to come since she have been seeing Clarence around town. Mary was single so she told Delilah that she could stay over at her home. Delilah arrived around 6:00 p.m.; it was just about to get dark. She and Mary sit around a while and talked, then they decided to get out and go into town. Mary decided that they would drive her car since she was more familiar with the town. It was very busy that night so they decided to go eat out and go to the fair tomorrow. Well, they decided to splurge a little so they went to this fancy restaurant called Ralph's. This place was famous for great seafood; Delilah loved seafood. It brought back memories of her an Clarence. Anyway as they were waiting to be seated; Mary noticed that Clarence and his wife were sitting in a corner near the back. Delilah looked at Mary and said," Is something wrong?" Mary said, as she cleared her throat, "Don't look now, but Clarence and his wife is sitting in the corner to the back." Delilah immediately said, "I can't stay here, I don't want him to see me." Mary said, "Ok, we can leave." Before they left, Delilah made sure she got a good look at Clarence's wife. While they drove looking for another restaurant, Mary asked Delilah was she o.k.; Delilah said, "Better then ever." Mary said, "What is that suppose to mean." Delilah said I know who my competition is." Mary said, are you still going to see him after he lied to you?" Delilah said, "Yes I love him." Mary could not believe her ears. Well, they arrived to their destination, Mary got out the car, Delilah said, "Go ahead I'll be just a minute." Delilah dialed Clarence's number, she let it rang until he picked up. He did not know who it was because she hit *67 to make it private. When Clarence answered, he said, "Hello". Delilah said, "Hi baby, how are you? He began fumbling for words, and began to act as if Delilah was a guy. Delilah told him that she was coming in town tonight and that she wanted to see him. He said abruptly, "Let me get back with you." Her heart was filled with all types of feelings, because she never realized how far she would go when a person hurts you to your heart. She had no intentions of getting with him at all. Meanwhile Mary and Delilah enjoyed their meal with a glass of wine and jazz music. Time goes by extremely fast when you are having a good time. After being there about 2 hours; they decided to call it a night. On the way back to Mary's home; Delilah's phone rings; it was Clarence. She let it ring until it stopped. Mary said, "Why is he calling you? Delilah told Mary what she had done. Mary was tickled about it. Anyways, Clarence called over and over but Delilah never answered the telephone. Well, today was the big day for the fair and Delilah was excited, but before they go, they will go have a girls day. They will go and get a manicure and a pedicure. While getting their nails and feet done, in walks Clarence's wife. Delilah hunched Mary and said, "Look who's here." Mary told Delilah; please don't make a scene. Delilah said, "I would not do such a thing, I'm a lady with class and style." Mary knew Clarence but she only met his wife a few times. She may not recognize her; so she thought. Well while they were sitting there, Clarence's wife said to Mary, "Don't I know you, she said aren't you Clarence's classmate; we met at the reunion last year." Mary said, "Yeah, you are Clarence's wife; good to see you." Clarence wife politely spoke to Delilah. Delilah was shocked, and said, "Hello. " As they talked a while, Delilah could see that Clarence's wife was a very nice person. Clarence wife asked what was their plans for today. They told her they were going to the fair and she asked could she hang out because Clarence was hanging with the men today. Mary told Clarence's wife to take her vehicle to her house and they all could ride together. It was the perfect day to go to the fair they all thought. Clarence called Delilah's phone, but not one time did she answer. They were really enjoying themselves at the fair; they even rode rides. Well, as they were about to get on another ride, Clarence called his wife and asked her where she was. She let him know that she was at the fair. He was very loud on the phone telling her he passed and saw her car parked at somebody's house and he accused her of cheating. She abruptly said, "Good bye Clarence." She had tears in her eyes, and said, "The nerve of him accusing me of cheating after all I have been through with him. " Mary and Delilah looked at each other in surprise. Mary said, "Do we need to take you to your car?" She said, "No; it's about time he get a dose of his own medicine." Mary said, "What does that mean?" She said, "I have been nothing but good to that man and all he done was cheat on me." Delilah felt really bad and sad at the same time. They stayed about another hour at the fair and then left. While in route to Mary's house, Clarence's wife was still ranting and raving about what Clarence had done. Well as they pulled up to Mary's house, there was Clarence sitting in his car waiting on his wife. Delilah's eyes got so big and she wanted to squat down in her seat but that may have made Clarence's wife a little suspicious. She was going to act as if she did not know Clarence or was she going to tell it all? When Clarence saw it was 3 women in the car, he played it off by saying, "Hey Hun, did you have a great time at the fair? She gave him a look out of this world. Mary got out of the car and he recognized her and spoke. When he saw Delilah get out of the car, he looked at shook his head on the sly as if please don't say anything. Mary introduced them as if it was their first time meeting. Clarence wife said her good-byes to Delilah and Mary and told Clarence she will see him when he gets home. After Clarence's wife drove off, Clarence did not know if Mary knew that he and Delilah was seeing each other; so he told Mary it was nice to see her and told Delilah it was nice meeting her. As soon as Clarence left, he called Delilah. The first thing he wanted to do was apologize. Delilah said, "So when were you going to tell me that you were married?" He said, I can explain, she said, "No need to." Delilah told Clarence that she, Mary and his wife will be spending more time together. Clarence told Delilah that she could not do that and what about their relationship. Delilah told Clarence that they can still have a relationship based on her terms. Clarence told her anything she wanted as long as his wife doesn't find out. Well Clarence had to figure out how he was going to see Delilah if she was becoming friends with his wife. Weeks had gone by and Delilah and Clarence haven't spoken. Delilah has been very upset due to finding out that Clarence was a married man. She and Mary still kept in touch on what was going on with Clarence. The rumor was going around that Clarence and his wife were getting a divorce. Delilah told Mary to keep her informed on it. It had been a long week and Delilah decided that she would spend the evening along to get her thoughts together. After work she decided to go to the grocery store to get some food and a bottle of wine. While at the grocery store, she spotted an old high school friend. They talked a little while and decided that they would keep in touch more so they exchanged numbers. Delilah went to the register to check out and there was this strange guy by the door watching her; it gave her the chills. Meanwhile she got her groceries and decided that she would wait until someone else goes out so she would not be out there alone. As she and another lady walked out she could see the gentlemen slowly walking behind them. She immediately turned around and said, "May I help you?" He said, "Do you have some change that you can spare? "Delilah said, "I may have something just one minute." Well, after putting her bags into the car, she got out her wallet and as she went to pull out some money, the gentlemen snatched her wallet and ran off. Delilah ran behind him, but could not catch him. She immediately got to her cell phone and called the police. When the officer arrived, she explained to him that all her information was in that wallet. Now Delilah was worried about staying home alone. The officer gave her reassurance that they will patrol the area. When she arrived home, she sat down to get herself together. She was now glad that she bought the wine after all. Later after she eat and get comfortable, she will call Mary. While Delilah was calling Mary, the other line beeped and it was Clarence. Delilah decided to take Clarence's call. She was very short and brief. After Clarence said what he had to say, Delilah explained to him about her purse being taken. Clarence wanted to know why Delilah did not call him. Delilah bluntly said, "Clarence, remember you are a married man." Clarence cleared his throat and said, “I’m sorry." Delilah said, “Well I will be going now, I have another phone call I need to make.” After hanging up, Delilah called Mary. Mary was glad to hear from her. Once Delilah told her the situation about her purse; Mary told Delilah that she will be there the weekend. That really made Delilah happy to hear; she and Mary have become good friends. It was getting late, so they said their good-byes. Delilah had to get up early and go to the Motor Vehicle place to get another Driver’s License. While she was there she received a text from Clarence saying they needed to talk and he will be coming there this weekend. Delilah did not respond to the text. As she sat there, it dawned on her that Mary was coming this weekend. Immediately she tried to call Clarence back, but there was no answer. She did not think about texting him because she had so much on her mind at the time. This weekend was normally the girl’s weekend out. Delilah decided to call Mary to see what she could do to help her. The phone rang about 3 times before Mary picked up. She was still asleep. Delilah told Mary what was going on and Mary said, “Clarence’s wife called and wanted to know if we were getting together this weekend; I told her I was going to your house; she wanted to know if she could come.” Delilah said, “Clarence is coming down too.” Mary said, “Why would you let Clarence come down knowing I was coming down?" She said, "He texted me and I tried calling him back but did not get an answer; that is why I'm calling you." Delilah realized this situation is more than she can handle. Delilah thought how this would look if everyone showed up at her house; how would she explain Clarence being there. Well it was getting closer to the weekend and Delilah decided that she refused to be stressed out behind a situation that is out of her control. Sometimes we have situations in life because of the things we settle for. Delilah decided to leave work early since her friends were coming over. She wants to make sure everything is clean and tidy. She had it nice and cozy for a girl's night for movies and popcorn. After freshening up, the doorbell rang; it was Mary and Clarence's wife. They hugged and she invited them in and told them to make themselves at home. Delilah continued to get dressed and let them know she would be out shortly. Clarence wife was very complementary about Delilah's home.

Delilah stepped into the room and asked if they wanted something to drink. Clarence's wife wanted a glass of water. After sitting and getting comfortable, Delilah let her guest know that they will be doing dinner, movie, and eat popcorn. Once they would eat dinner they would all get into their pajamas and watch a movie and popcorn. That sounds good to Mary and Clarence's wife. They decided to watch a love movie. Well after the movie was over they decided to have a girls talk. Delilah opened the floor and said that she was grateful for such good friends; and she became teary eyed. Mary and Clarence's wife immediately came and put their arms around Delilah. Mary said, "Delilah is something wrong?" She said, "I'm just overwhelmed with all that has happened." They reassured her that everything was going to be alright. While Clarence was in route to Delilah's house he decided to call his wife. When Clarence's wife phone rang, she said, "Excuse me this is my husband." Delilah just went into shock mode wondering if Clarence was really coming to her house. After Clarence's wife came back into the room she said, "Clarence said he had a business meeting out of town and the he will be back on Sunday. Delilah immediately got up and went into her bedroom to call Clarence; he never picked up his phone. She could not get so nervous that she would give herself away that something was really wrong. Well the night went on and it was time for girls' pillow talk. Clarence's wife decided that she wanted to break the ice by first letting Delilah know she thanked her for allowing her to come into her home. Oh, this is really making Delilah feel guilty. She told them how she and Clarence have been going through so much because he has been cheating on her since they have been married. She said, "I'm really thinking about asking Clarence for a divorce; but before I do, I will make him pay for everything he put me through." She said, "My lawyer said I would have a better case if I could catch him cheating." A thought came to Delilah because she was really hurt by Clarence. Well by that time, Delilah's phone rang; it was Clarence. She said, "Excuse me; I need to take this call." Mary did not know how to feel being that she was Clarence's wife friend and also Delilah's friend. How will she explain that she knew all along that Delilah was seeing Clarence? Anyway, Mary and Clarence's wife could hear Delilah yelling on the phone. When she came back into the room, you could tell she had been crying. They both said, "Is there anything we can do?" She said "No, this is something that I must take care of myself." She said, "I need to go out for a while, I will be back." After she left, Clarence's wife was very concerned for Delilah. Mary said, "She will be alright and you will too." Clarence's wife said, "What do you mean by that?" Mary said, "She is going through the same thing you are going through." Clarence's wife said, "I did not know Delilah was seeing someone." Delilah met up with Clarence at the Library parking lot. Clarence told Delilah how much he missed her and that he was sorry about not telling her about his wife, but he was going to. Delilah asked him did he love his wife and Clarence said, "I wouldn't be here with you if I did." Delilah said," Why didn't you tell me you were married and give me a chance to make a choice whether I wanted to be in this type of relationship or not." Clarence said, "I fell for you so quick that I didn't think about it, but I was going to get around to it." Delilah was so outdone she could hardly keep herself together. She then said, "Do you want to come to the house:" Clarence eyes lit up and he said, "I thought you would never ask." He gave her a hug and went to his car. As they arrived at her home, she waited by her car so they could walk in together. She had mixed feelings about this situation, but doing the right thing was not a option. The pain that Clarence made her feel was indescribable. Finally Delilah turned the key in the door and went in. Mary and Clarence's wife were sitting on the couch watching a movie. They said, "Come on girl, you are missing a good movie." Delilah did not answer, so they turned around and there was Clarence. His wife said, "What are you doing here; and how do you? Clarence's wife ran hysterically into the room and Clarence went after her. She said, "How long have you been cheating with her? Clarence said for a while, but I don't love her, I love you." She said, "I need you to tell her that you don't love her." They went into the other side and Delilah just stood there in a blank stare. While crying hysterically, Clarence wife insisted he tell Delilah. Clarence said, “Delilah I don’t love you, I love my wife and it is over between us.” Delilah said, “That’s fine, it’s been over with you, but when I heard your wife stating she wanted to catch you in the act, I could not let this opportunity pass me by. Clarence said, “What is she talking about?” His wife said, “I hired a lawyer and he said if I could catch you in adultery then I have good grounds for divorce.” Clarence said, “So Delilah this was”; before he could finish, she said, "you right, a set up.” She and Clarence’s wife gave a high five and Mary opened the door for him and told him to hit the road. The mind and heart is nothing to play around with. See in life there will be things and people that may do things to you, but what goes around comes around. Unless you have a heart change you will not have a mind change.

10 *YOUR CHOICE!*

Our flesh is weak but our spirit is strong; It is time to let go

to live and move on.

God is in control and He knows what is best

He will keep you at peace and give you rest.

Our trust is in him that is all we

know; He is from eternity to eternity and the world should know.

He will pick you up when your are feeling down;

He will set you free from the things that have you bound.

He is the answer for the world today; But no one's listening their just going their way.

There are only two places you can go; If no one tells you, you will never know.

Heaven or Hell which one you choose; If you choose wrong you will surely lose.

He went away to prepare us a place; He left us here to finish this race.

The race of life is what we call it to be; But he gave his son so we could be free

You have heaven to gain and hell to lose; Be wise which one do you choose.

Ready or not he's coming soon; after that day the world is doomed

Do you tell people Jesus is your father; Or you go every day and just don't bother.

To tell them he can change their lives; You can only serve one; God or the Devil so please be wise.

Some people say it don't matter at all; the day will come when you have to answer the call.

What will you say to the one who knows it all?

See your destination is chosen while you live; So in the end you have no excuse to give.

There is a hell to miss and a heaven to gain in the end you have no one else to blame but yourself !

11

Are you Dressed for the Wedding?

This gentleman was a very wise old soul. He came in contact with persons of all different races because it don't matter the color of your skin you are either going to the wedding or you're not! We should know by now that everyone is different. There is a reason for every situation. When people grow old, the saying is that, "People forget about you." Well in this case it is not so, this gentlemen may have been by himself but it seemed as though he was forgotten about, but he knew better. Just because a person don't say the things in a way in which we think they should say them, does not make that person wrong. The bible says;" Only a fool utters all his mind, but a wise man keep it in till afterwards" **(Proverbs 29:11).** Don't Matter your skin color; "For the Son of Man came to save that which was lost" **(Matthew 18:11).**

We live in a society today as to where if a person is not doing what we are doing we call them strange and when we don't know a person we tend to judge them. Well there was this elderly gentlemen living on a back street near an alley; everyone called him Mr. Pete. He has been living there his entire life. It felt very creepy if you walked pass his house day or night. Every now and then you would see Mr. Pete walking to the store or just sitting on his porch. Mr. Pete normally speaks to people along his path. One day as he was on his way to the store, he passed a young man and said, "I'm going to a wedding." The young man snickered and shook his head as if he was saying that old man is crazy. Meanwhile he arrived at the store and when he get in close contact to a person, he would say; "I'm going to a wedding." People would just look at him and brush him off as if he had not said anything. People looked at him as if he was nobody; and he knew that but what they did not know that he has been around a long time and had plenty of wisdom. There was a school in the neighborhood down the road from where Mr. Pete lived. One day he was walking as usual through the neighborhood and one of the young guys said, "Don't tell us, you're going to a wedding." Mr. Pete said, "Yes I'm, are you going". The young man said," sure let us know when it will be." Mr. Pete kept on walking and whistling along the way. He knew the young man was taking what he said lightly.

Most elderly people tend to walk with their heads hanging down. While Mr. Pete continued on his journey, he came to an intersection. As usual, he waited for the light to give him the right away to walk across. While walking across there came a car of young kids who ran through the red light. Being up in age, Mr. Pete was unable to move out of the way in time. The car hit Mr. Pete knocking him to the ground. Living in times like these people will not get involved in situations that don't concern them. Well, the car stopped a few hundred yards away to make sure Mr. Pete was alright and not dead. When they saw Mr. Pete rise up, they left the scene. Mr. Pete could not move his legs, but he waived for someone to help him. There came a young man from around the corner who walked up and said, "Are you alright?" Mr. Pete said, "I was hit by some kids and they drove away." The young man said, "I will go in the store and call 911." With a light breath due to shock, Mr. Pete said, "Thank you;" before he passed out. When the paramedics arrived the young man was still there with Mr. Pete. The police arrived on the scene and got a statement from the young man that Mr. Pete had given him. The young man asked the paramedics the hospital in which they were taking Mr. Pete so he could check on him later. Mr. Pete end up having surgery due to a broken leg. After he woke up in the recovery room; there was the young man sitting at his bedside. Mr. Pete still under sedation; said, “Am I at the wedding?” The young man said, “No, you are in the hospital; you were hit by a car." He then asked the young man, “Who are you?” The young man said, “My name is Todd.” Mr. Pete said, “Have we met before?” Todd said, “No, I saw you needed help and I helped you.” Mr. Pete said, “You must be one of the ones who are going to the wedding.” He said, “What wedding?” He said, "Son one day remind me to tell you about the wedding.” That made Todd kind of curious because Mr. Pete said the same thing earlier. Todd thought to himself, this man surely could not be getting married at his age. The nurse walked into the room to let Mr. Pete know that visiting hours were about to end. Todd left his name and number with the nurse to let him know when Mr. Pete will be released and he will pick him up and make sure he gets home safely. As Todd was driving in route to his home, the wedding stayed on his mind. He decided that he was going to do a little research on the wedding. He thought about it; he did not have Mr. Pete’s last name so he could not look up anything. He decided when he picks Mr. Pete up from the hospital he will get more information. A week had passed and the time had come for Mr. Pete to be released from the hospital; he sat near the door waiting for his transportation to come.

Mr. Peter was not too surprised to see Todd; he knew there was something special about that young man. As they were in route to Mr. Pete's home; Todd asked Mr. Pete if there were anything he needed to do before he brought him home. Mr. Pete said, "Son, I just appreciate you taking time out of your busy schedule and helping me; that says a lot." That really touched Todd's heart, as he teared up. He told Mr. Pete that he was just glad he could be of help. Todd began to tell Mr. Pete how he grew up in a house where his father expected perfection from him and that is why he tries so hard to do the right things. Mr. Pete said, "I have been around for 80 years and I could never do everything right." Todd said, "My father did." Mr. Pete said, "No he did not; it was only in your eyes he did." Do you know anything about the bible Mr. Pete asked Todd? Not really, see we did not go to church because my father was a very strict and proud man and said he will never depend on anyone. Mr. Pete asked Todd, "Do you believe that?" Todd said "I don't know what to believe; I just know you needed help and I was there so I helped you" Mr. Pete now sees that he was destined to meet

Todd; he was his next project.

When they drove into the drive way, Todd got out to help Mr. Pete out of the car. Now that Mr. Pete had broken his leg he was going to need some help around the house until he gets better. Before Mr. Pete could get the words out, Todd said, "I will stop by after work for a few weeks until you can get back to moving around again." Mr. Pete said, "You know son, you are one of a kind." Mr. Pete watched as Todd got into his car and drove out of sight. As the evening passed on, Mr. Pete decided to go to turn in early, but he decided he wanted to do something special for Todd first. As he laid in bed, he began to pray; "Lord, I want you to bless Todd for his labor and that I will be able to pour into his life the things that you have me to say; help him to understand the natural things as well as the spiritual things in Jesus name; amen and he fell asleep. Mr. Pete realized that he was old and he needed to leave what he has learned in his years with someone who can pass it on. On the way home Todd was in deep thought, he realized that his father and Mr. Pete were totally opposite. He sees how Mr. Pete just accepted him for who he was. He had a good feeling about this relationship that he and Mr. Pete has begun. The next morning was very pleasant; the birds chirping as the sun peaking out. Todd had to be at work very early that morning. When he arrived at work, he got out of his vehicle whistling and smiling. He went into the break room to put his lunch in his locker and one of his co-workers said," Why are you so happy today?" He said, "I met someone that I have not known for a long time, but it seems like it." He is around 80 years old; when he said that his friend said, "He is like your grandfather." Todd said, "No he is very different in a good way and he said he is going to a wedding; but he never said who's wedding." His friend said, "When you find out let me know"; and he walked away laughing.

Soon after work was over Todd could not wait to get in the car and be on his way to Mr. Pete's house. He was really excited about what Mr. Pete was going to tell him about the wedding. Well as he drove into the driveway, he could see Mr. Pete sitting at the table as if he was waiting for him to get there. Anyway, as soon as he knocked on the door, Mr. Pete invited him in. Todd sat at the table across from Mr. Pete. Mr. Pete asked him how his day went and Todd told him it was good. He then said, "My co-worker and I had a discussion about what you said about going to a wedding." My co-worker was really tickled about it; he wants to know more about it and I told him I would let him know once I found out more." Mr. Pete said, "It is so much to tell you I don't know where to start." He started off by asking Todd have he heard about Jesus. Todd said, "I use to hear my parents talk about Jesus, and how he is coming soon." Mr. Pete said, "Well do you believe that? Todd said, "Maybe one day I will, but right now I'm too young to be thinking about that, so he thought. Mr. Pete said, "So are you ready to die?" Todd said, "No I have too much to do in my life." Mr. Pete then went on to explain to Todd; this life we live is not our own and tomorrow is not promised to us. God sent his son Jesus to die so that we might live. Todd said, how do you know these things?" The bible tells us what we need to know about Jesus. We are born physically by our earthly parents which is temporary because one day they may leave us physically by death because everything that is temporary is subject to change; but with God everything is eternal; it last forever. Todd was sitting there trying to remember everything Mr. Pete was telling him. He found it to be very interesting. Todd said, "What about the wedding? Mr. Pete said, "Oh you can't go to the wedding unless you are invited and once you are invited you must accept the invitation; everything that I tell you is leading up to the wedding. Todd thought that to be very odd because you have to go through all that just to go to a wedding. Well it was getting late and Todd had to go to work the next day.

The next day at work his co-worker said, "So are you going to the wedding?" Todd told his co-worker the conversation with Mr. Pete was very interesting and that maybe he should think about going with him one afternoon to hear what Mr. Pete has to say. His co-worker said, "I might take you up on that offer one day." Meanwhile there was a calmness that came over Todd; he thought to himself; "There just might be something to what Mr. Pete is saying." Seem as though the older people tend to talk more because they have been around a lot longer. They have been through so much during their life and they have a lot of wisdom. Todd continued to visit Mr. Pete as he was still recovering from his leg injury. Mr. Pete was recovering better than expected. When a person is older the healing process tends to take longer, but not in this case. Todd told Mr. Pete that he was informing a co-worker about the things that he was learning from him. Mr. Pete face lit up because he realizes that Todd is being a witness and not even realizing it. Mr. Pete decided on tomorrow that he will began to walk a few blocks to get his leg stronger and get back to normal. When you are an early riser, the morning seems to come very early. Even though Mr. Pete woke up early he did not leave the house until around noon. Mr. Pete always goes his same route passing by the recreational center. The young kids that normally make fun of Mr. Pete noticed he was not quite himself that day. They were very respectful and just spoke to him. Mr. Pete waived and said, "I'm going to a Wedding." One of the guys said, "Why does that old man always say that?" His friend said, "I don't know, but one day I will get a chance to ask him when he is feeling better. As Mr. Pete got further up the road, a car came passing by very slow and there were some young kids with the windows down. They said, "Hey sir, how are you doing?" He said, "I'm fine just trying to get better." They said, "What happen to you?" He said, "I was hit by a hit and run driver." One of the young men said in a whispering voice; "That look like person we hit the other week'' Then all of a sudden the car sped off, but Mr. Peter had already seen their faces. Mr. Pete was going to contact the police, but decided that he was still alive and he had another plan. Getting those individuals to the wedding was more important than seeing them incarcerated; they may not get the opportunity to go. Mr. Pete finally got back to his home and the mailman was putting his mail in his mailbox, but when he saw Mr. Pete he handed him the mail. He finally got into the house and sat at the table to go through his mail. While going through the mail; there was a knock at the door. Mr. Peter does not normally have visitors. Mr. Peter had one of those closed in porches with a screen door. When he got to the door, he looked and it was one of the young men who were in the car earlier, but Mr. Pete did not acknowledge it. The young man said he wanted to speak with Mr. Pete for a moment. Mr. Pete asked the young man if he wanted to come in. The young man was surprised Mr. Pete invited him in. When the young man got into the house, he was looking around as if he was in amazement. He said, "I just wanted to apologize for what happened to you a few weeks ago. Mr. Pete said, "I forgive you." He said, How could you do that so easily." Mr. Pete said, "I have been around a long time and at my age, it is easier to forgive than to hold grudges." The young man noticed a sign on the wall and it said, "I'm going to a wedding are you going?" That stood out to the young man, so he said, "What do you mean by going to a wedding." He said, like I told another young man; "The only way to go to the wedding you must be invited and you must accept the invitation. The young man asked when was the wedding going to take place. Mr. Pete told him it could happen any day. That kind of puzzled the young man. He starting thinking the old man was senile or something. He then abruptly told Mr. Pete he had to leave. As he was leaving, Mr. Pete said you and your friends should come back and I will tell you more about the wedding.

The young man said, “Maybe we will.” The young man was very confused at this moment because he didn’t want his friends to know what he had done. He did not want to stand out as a wimp.

Later that evening as usual, Todd came over to check on Mr. Pete, he told Todd about the visit he had today with one of the young men in the car. Mr. Pete said, “I did not alert the police, I forgave them.” Todd thought Mr. Pete was crazy in a sense because no one normally would does such a thing. Mr. Pete told Todd that he rather see those young man go to the wedding instead of being incarcerated. Todd said, “Mr. Pete you are not going to a wedding.” Mr. Pete said, “You will see, but you must believe it will happen.” Todd asked Mr. Pete; “Who is going to be at this wedding?” Mr. Pete said, “Everyone who accepted the invitation." Todd said, "When did you start giving out invitations?" Mr. Pete said, "I have been giving out invitations for over 40 years." Now Todd really was puzzled; he thought, who would give invitations out for all those years and never get married? Mr. Pete offered Todd something to eat, but he was going to get something on his way home. While in route home, Todd stopped at this small burger place. Since the drive thru line was so long he decided to go inside. While he stood in line to order his food, there sat 3 guys at a table talking. He over heard one of the gentlemen saying he went to a man's house who was talking about a wedding. Todd then realized that was the 3 young men who left Mr. Pete in the street after running over him. He continued in line and after he received his food he stopped at the table. He told them he could not help overhearing their conversation about the Mr. Pete. Todd explained to them how they could have killed Mr. Pete and spend the rest of their lives in jail; but instead Mr. Pete chose to forgive them. The young men were surprised Todd knew who they were. Todd told them he was the one who rescued Mr. Pete after they ran over him and drove off. When Todd got out of sight, the two friends said, "Why didn't you tell us this was the man you was talking about?" As the young man tried to explain, the two friends got up and walked off. Now the young man kind of hated he even said something to them. Days had gone by and the young man had not spoken to his two friends; he was feeling kind of down. He needed someone to talk to so he decided to go back to Mr. Pete's house. Mr. Pete as usual was sitting on the porch. Before he knocked; Mr. Pete said," Come on in son." He said, "I have been expecting you." The young man said, " How did you know I would come back?" He then said, " Sometimes when you do the right thing you have to stand alone." Mr. Pete knew that this young man's heart was right if he came to apologize for he and his friends; it also showed how he cared about other people. The young man explained to Mr. Pete what happened and Mr. Pete said, "True friends stick together thru anything." That got the young man to thinking; "Maybe they are not my friends." Everyone that smiles in you face is not your friend. Mr. Pete and the young man was about to have dinner when Todd knocked on the door. Mr. Pete said, "It's open, come on in; we were just about to have dinner, care to join us?" Todd joined them; it kind of surprised Mr. Pete that he did. Todd explained to the young man that he was not trying to come down hard on he and his friends, but wanted them to know that things could have been very different, but because of Mr. Pete's heart; it was a different outcome. In life everything we do is a choice. The young man was very attentive and it got him to thinking about, what if Mr. Pete would have died. Even though he was not the one driving he still would have been at fault just being in the vehicle. That really hit home for the young man. He began to cry and began apologizing to Mr. Pete again. Mr. Pete said, "Son I have forgiven you." The young man said, "So are you still mad?" Mr. Pete explained; "When someone forgives you, they no longer hold it against you." The young man got up and just hugged Mr. Pete as if he did not want to let go. Mr. Pete patted him on the back as a father would do a son; and told him; "It's going to be alright." That really calmed the young man down. After they ate and continued talking a while longer, then it was time to go. Since Todd and the young man were leaving at the same time, Todd offered the young man a ride home; he accepted.

While in route to the young man's home; he and Todd talked. Todd told the young man that he was glad that he went to Mr. Pete for advice because he felt his friends were leading him down the wrong path. Todd abruptly said, "What do you think about Mr. Pete and this wedding?" The young man said, "I believe him". Todd was surprised, he said, "Really?" The young man said, "Well he has been around a long time and why would he wait until he get this age to start telling stories." Todd thought to himself, that makes sense. They kept driving and finally the young man said, "You can let me out here and I will walk the rest of the way." Todd said, "No, I can take you all the way home." The young man was like, "O.K." They drove for about 15 more minutes and the young man told Todd to turn at the next light; Todd said, "I live about 2 blocks from here." The young man said, "Wow what a small world." As they drove up in front of the house, there were a lot of people standing around. When the young man opened the door and got out, Todd rolled down his window to say bye, but someone yelled out, "Get out of here." Todd ignored them and asked the young man, "Are you going to be alright." He said, "Yeah." As Todd pulled off he was looking in his mirror and he saw some guy knock the young man down and began hitting him. Todd wanted to turn around, but he felt it was a rough kind of environment. He decided to call the police. Todd stayed a distance until the police arrived and he watched to see what the police was going to do. The police end up taking the young man downtown out of the environment. Todd followed them to the police station. He asked the police officer if he could see the young man; only for 15 minutes. The young man told Todd he was in foster care and he really did not have anywhere to stay; he was just from place to place. Todd became teary eyed because it touched his heart and he knew he had to do something. The officer told the young man they could only let him stay overnight, but they will have to let him go back on the streets due to him being 18. Todd told the young man that he may be able to let him stay at his place until he could help him get somewhere to stay. The young man agreed and left with Todd. While driving, the young man said, "How could you do something like this for a total stranger. Todd said, I have learned a lot from Mr. Pete." I have never had a role model at home, but Mr. Pete has a good heart and I want my heart to be just like his." The young man said under his breath, "Thank you." This was going to be a long night because Todd is not use to having someone staying with him and barely know them. He gave the young man blanket and he slept on the sofa. Meanwhile, Todd had to call Mr. Pete to tell him what happened. Even though Mr. Pete was an early bird; he still answered the telephone. After telling Mr. Pete what happened; Mr. Pete told Todd that was a good thing he had done. Todd told Mr. Peter before hanging up, " It's all because of you Mr. Pete that my heart is changing." Mr. Pete just sat on the phone, and then said, "Goodnight son." The young man heard what Todd said; covered his head and went sound to sleep. The only book people can read sometimes is you. Be careful the things you do and say around people because you just might be a role model.

Morning had come and Todd was in route to work. He left everything that the young man needed written on the tablet sitting on the counter. Todd also told the young man that he was going by Mr. Pete when he get off of work to check on him. Meanwhile Mr. Pete as usual taking his walk around noon time; so he came to the recreational center where kids are always playing sports. This particular day; no one was there playing sports, maybe because it had rained earlier. Anyway the young man two friends were walking this time. Mr. Pete said, "I'm going to a Wedding, do you want to go?" The two young men immediately knew that was the gentlemen that they hit. They remembered the conversation their friend had told them. They started to run off; but Mr. Pete told them to come to him. You can see they were kind of nervous; guilt will do you that way. Mr. Pete asked them to sit down because he wanted to talk to them. Mr. Pete wanted to know what made them drive off and not help him. One of the young men said, "I'm sorry." The other young man which was the driver said; "I don't have any driver's license." Mr. Pete asked him whose car was he driving; he said, "it was stolen." Now that made the whole situation change. Mr. Pete said, “If you would have killed me; the person name on the car may have been at fault." He said, “I will have to report this to the police." The boys began to tear up and begged Mr. Pete not to turn them in. Mr. Pete told them that the truth will set them free. The boys did not understand what Mr. Pete was saying. He explained to them, "Once you tell the truth, you don't have to lie anymore." Mr. Pete decided that the young men will tell the car was stolen, but not that they hit him. The young men were amazed and said, "You would do that for us." Mr. Pete said, "Everyone deserves another chance." The Young men asked Mr.

Pete if he would go with them to turn themselves in for stealing the vehicle. Mr. Pete agreed to go with them. It was almost time for Todd to get off of work; so Mr. Pete headed back home and will meet the young men on tomorrow. The young men decided that they would walk Mr. Pete home. So as they were walking, one of the young men said; our friend told us you were going to a wedding; so what wedding are you going to? Mr. Pete said, "In order to go you must be invited and you must accept the invitation. The young men said, "Is our friend going"? Mr. Pete said, "He hasn't accepted the invitation yet." They said, "If he go we will go." Mr. Pete said, "Is that a promise?" they agreed. Todd pulled up the same time the two young men were at Mr. Pete's house. They immediately recognized each other. They said, "Hello again." Mr. Pete said, "Do you'll know each other?" They explained how they met at the burger joint. They then said, "Have you seen our friend; we sure do miss him." Todd said, "You two were wrong the way you treated your friend; friends don't do each other that way." One of the young men said, "I wish I could see him again to tell him how sorry I'm." Todd did not say anything about the young man staying with him in front of his friends. They need to learn what true friends really are. The two young men said their good-byes to Mr. Pete and Todd. Mr. Pete yelled out; "Don't make this your last time coming by." Todd and Mr. Pete went into the house and he and Todd talked as usual. With Todd being off work on tomorrow; Mr. Pete asked Todd if he would be willing to take him down to the police station with the two young men; Todd agreed. The next day Todd showed up to Mr. Pete he had the young man in the car with him. Mr. Pete knew this would happen and this would give him the opportunity to talk with all 3; by the way the young man had to turn himself in also. By the time they were getting out the car the other two young men arrived. They did not see their other friend at first. When he stepped out the car; the other two friends ran and embraced him. They wanted to know where he had been and that they missed him. Anyways, they all got into the car and headed down to the police station. When they arrived; Mr. Pete informed him that he will do the talking. After each person met with the officer separately, the owner of the vehicle decided that they would not be pressing charges due to these were teenagers and he remembered being one also. Mr. Pete shook the owner's hand and told him he appreciated him doing that for them. Meanwhile the three friends embraced each other and vowed to never do anything like that again. The two friends told their other friend that if he was going to the wedding, they were going to.

The young man said, "First we have to find out where the wedding is going to be." Mr. Pete, just smiled and said, "It won't be long. " Todd was so amazed at what just happened; he could not believe it. He felt as if being around Mr. Pete makes good things happen. When God's anointing is on your life things happen. The three young men and Todd began meeting up at Mr. Pete's house at least twice a week. Mr. Pete really began to enjoy the company. Well the last time they were at Mr. Pete he had a slight cold with a deep cough. Todd was concerned about him, but Mr. Pete said he was alright and was taking something for it. Anyway weeks went by and everything was going pretty good. The three young men normally go to Mr. Pete before Todd comes. Well, they went to Mr. Pete and noticed that the door was still closed and that was not like Mr. Pete. They knocked, but no one answered. The three friends became concerned so they called Todd. Todd told them that Mr. Pete had not been feeling well, so he is probably sleeping more. About 15 minutes later, Mr. Pete came to the door and sat down at the table as usual. The three friends; got up from outside the gate and went to the door. Mr. Pete offered them in as usual. He was a little disoriented due to just waking up out of a deep sleep. The friends kept an eye on Mr. Pete because he was not his usual self. Todd finally arrived and breathes a sigh of relief to see Mr. Pete. While they were there; Mr. Pete told them he had something to tell them. He told them he was dying. The friends and Todd just sat there in shock. Todd said, "How is that and you are doing so well." Mr. Pete said, "I have known this for quite some time." The three friends began to cry; and say, "But we don't want you to die." He said, "It's not your will, but God's will." He told them; I have lived my life and I have told you things that you can share with others. Remember God does not give everything to one person; He always has someone else he can use; you just have to be a willing vessel. Mr. Pete said, "Oh, that wedding I have been talking about; I have been invited and I have accepted the invitation. Todd and the three friends looked puzzled; Mr. Pete told them to come by tomorrow and he will tell them the rest. Todd found that strange because he never is eager for anyone to leave; but they respected his wishes. After everyone left, Mr. Pete prayed and asked God to protect Todd and the three friends when he is no longer here. Also that the preacher will make the funeral so simple that people would be accepting the invitation to the wedding.

Well the next day was not the day that they met at Mr. Pete's house, but Todd was going by anyway after the disturbing news Mr.

Pete gave on yesterday once he get off work. The recreational center was crowed as usual and everyone knew Mr. Pete and his walking pattern. Well that particular he did not walk. Some people found if strange because they were use to seeing him. There was a neighbor that lived a few houses down; got a little concerned when he did not see Mr. Pete pass by his house; so he decided to go to his home. He knocked and no one answered; that concerned him. He decided to call the police since he just could not break in his home. The police arrived on the scene and knocked on the door. Since no one answered, the police had to use extra force to enter the home. There they found Mr. Pete in his bed; he had passed away in his sleep. They called the corner to come and view the body and give the time of death. When Todd got off work he went on over as usual to Mr. Pete's house, but they had a lock on the gate. He went down to the nearest neighbor and he told him Mr. Pete passed away. Todd had to take a deep breath and sit down. He was lost for words and how was he going to tell the three friends. Anyway the three friends were always at the recreational center telling everyone about the wedding that they were going to. Todd went to the center and they looked at Todd and could see something was wrong. Todd said; "It's Mr. Pete; he passed away today." The friends cried, "No, not Mr. Pete; we loved him; he took time up with us; he told us the truth; they cried hysterically. After getting through much pain they had to pull themselves together ;after all they were the only family he had. When people start noticing that they haven't been seeing Mr. Pete around they were concerned. The word got around that Mr. Pete had passed away. People felt kind of bad because all they would do is make fun of the old man and mock him. People in the neighborhood may have not said much to the old man, but now that he was not around they missed seeing him. A lot of people got together and decided that they would go to the funeral.

Well today was the day to lay Mr. Pete to rest. The old man was dressed very nice at his funeral. Mr. Pete had all his arrangements in order. Mr. Pete wanted the funeral director to preach the funeral. The funeral director went on to say, "He finally made it to his destination." The preacher said, "Before I preach his home going, would anyone like to say a few words about Mr. Pete. The young guy that snickered at Mr. Pete said, " I would like to say that I never really got a chance to know Mr. Pete, but he told me that he was going to a wedding, but I never got a chance to ask him what he meant by that statement." He seemed like a nice person, but I now realize that when you don't take the time to get to know someone you may be missing out on an opportunity for them to teach you something; I just regret not getting to know him." The preacher went on to say; "Anyone who came in contact with Mr. Pete knew he was going to a wedding; this is how you get dressed for the wedding. No matter how dressed up you are for the wedding if you don't accept the invitation; you are not getting in. One day Jesus is coming back for his bride; which is the church. Will you be dressed for the wedding? See in order to get dressed you first must be washed in the blood of Jesus. Jesus came and died so we can go and live. **Well it is simple; Roman 10:9** *****If though confess with thy mouth the Lord Jesus and believe in thy heart that God has raised him from the dead thy shall be saved *******Romans: 10:10** (For with the heart man believeth unto righteousness and with the mouth confession is made unto salvation). After the call was made, many went and accepted Jesus as Lord and Savior. Todd and the young men went up because they wanted to say something about Mr. Pete. Todd said, "Mr. Pete was a wise man and we promised him that we would go to the wedding; we now realize that if we don't go to the wedding we will never see Mr. Pete again, so I would like to accept Jesus in my heart." After that the other three young men agreed with Todd and accepted Jesus also. The things that Mr. Pete had been telling them finally made sense to them. Todd snickered and said, "All the time he was talking about a Heavenly Wedding. From that day forward their lives were never the same. When they closed Mr. Pete's casket it read: "You may be physically dressed for this present funeral but are you spiritually dressed for the future wedding? " **SEE YOU AT THE WEDDING!!!!!!!!**

ABOUT THE AUTHOR

I'm from a small town called Vinton, Louisiana. I have a wonderful husband who has supported me; we've been married for 23 years. I have a love for people and have learned how to enjoy life. I also walk in my uniqueness that God has given me.

Made in the USA
Coppell, TX
22 October 2021